ALMOND

and the deep blue sea

Jim Hawkins

Amazon

ISBN-13: 9798407963646
ISBN-10: 1477123456

Cover design by: Art Painter
Library of Congress Control Number: 2018675309
Printed in the United States of America

*To my darling Gillie, with love and thanks for
keeping me going, for reading with painful eyes,
and for being you.*

*With huge thanks to Lesley Ann Hoy Mouzakiti,
without whose vast local knowledge this novel
would not have been possible.*

*And also to the people of the village of Agios
Stefanos in north west Corfu. They have
made my many stays there a joy; their warmth
and friendliness is beyond compare.*

CHAPTER ONE

I was sitting in *The Prince* eating chicken, mushroom and tarragon pie with mash and gravy, an order of chips on the side, and a pint of top-notch Harvey's Best Bitter, right in the heart of Stoke Newington in Norff Lon'on, minding my own business, when she walked in.

She was classy – maybe mid-forties, like me – shoulder-length brown hair above a leather jacket, black top and jeans. She had a small silver cross on a chain round her neck. This area's not like it was when I was brought up near here. I'm not saying the girls weren't great, but they just somehow didn't have the polish, if you know what I mean.

This pub used to sell curled-up cheese sandwiches in white bread, and Watney's, for fuck's sake. Then it went seriously downhill and they ripped all the old stuff out and turned it into a plastic nightmare. Then it closed. A new lot bought it up, and made it look like a traditional East End pub, only with class. No more old cheese sandwiches. Salmon and risotto, and oysters, and pies like this with mash, gravy and decent beer.

And classy birds like the one who'd just walked in.

She spoke to Dom, the good-looking deputy manager, and walked across to me.

'Johnny Almond?'

I pointed at the chair across from me. 'Have a chip.'

She sat down and took two chips from the bowl. 'Chips AND mash?' she said.

I shrugged. 'I like chips. I like mash. Is that a problem?'

'I'm a doctor. Officially I should say that's not a great diet – but really I'm more interested in what you do than what you eat.'

'Have another chip, doctor. I might have a blood-pressure problem.'

'Why's that?'

'It's pretty recent. Why does what I do interest you?'

'I thought they served greens with the pie?'

'I told them not to bother. Are you from the diet Flying Squad?'

She laughed. Then she leaned forward.

'My sister's in deep shit. I would like you to help.'

'Drink?' I put my hand up and Dom raised his eyebrows and nodded. "Mind if I carry on eating my cardiac arrest while you tell me?'

'I feel duty bound to eat another chip for the sake of your health,' she said. I pushed the bowl towards her, and carried on eating. She watched the awkward way I cut the pie crust with my left hand. You bloody try it. The best I could do was hold the fork loosely in my right hand and use the knife with my left. Most of the time I eat fork foods, like curry; I'm not American and can shovel food in with the fork in my left hand. One-handed chopping is not very pretty to watch.

Dom came over and put a glass of pink stuff on her side of the table. She smiled up at him and said 'Thank you, Dom. Maybe Mr Almond would like another pint?'

I nodded.

'You actually *like* Campari Soda? Tastes like bloody cough mixture!'

'Maybe I like cough mixture.' She took a sip and smiled, her dark brown eyes crinkling in a way that made me think she could practise her bedside manner beside my bed any time she felt like it. Fat chance.

I put my fork on the plate and rested my hands on the table. She leaned forward. 'May I look at it? Your hand?'

'Be my guest.' She leaned forward and examined my hand closely. 'You can touch. But then, doctors don't touch anybody since we got the Covid plague, do they?'

'How long ago?'

'Five months – give or take.'

'How did it happen?'

I waited until she looked up from my hand. 'Do you usually do consultations in the pub?' I asked.

She shook her head.

'Nor do I', I said, and added 'Usually.'

'Sorry. It's unusual, so I was curious about the damage and the treatment. It was rude of me – professional hazard.'

'That,' I said, pointing to the big scar across my

hand about an inch behind the knuckles, 'is *my* professional hazard. Machete. We call it a defensive injury. I put my arm up to protect my face.'

'You're army?'

'Police. I was a DI in the Met. I made a stupid mistake and went in on my own when I should have had ten guys from Armed-Response do it for me. Totally against the regs. Like I say – stupid. Very stupid. Very painfully stupid.'

'We all make mistakes.'

'The only good thing was my young woman detective sergeant was waiting outside because I told her to. She could have been killed.'

'So could you.'

'Yep. But I wasn't.'

'You need lots of healthy food and vitamins. Fruit. Calcium to help your bones knit. B12 to promote nerve growth. Fish. Pie, mash and chips is not really ideal. And you really should stop smoking. But I expect they told you that.'

'How do you know I smoke?'

She laughed. Dom walked over with another pint and put it on the table. Usually he was chatty, but he was keeping a low profile because he obviously thought I was on the pull.

'Cheers, mate,' I said.

She looked up at him. 'I'll have another Campari. And I'll get Mr Almond's supper.'

Dom nodded and walked away. 'You're a detective. How would you tell if somebody smoked?' she asked.

'Nicotine stains.'

'Right.'

'Listen, doctor. If I could hold a fag in my right hand without it hurting like fuck I'd count that as a big step forward. By the way, I don't even know your name.'

'Maria. Doctor Maria Rogers.'

'Johnny Almond. NHS number nine two five seven eight three eight six one. Now, tell me about your sister, Doctor Rogers.'

'In a moment. Have you got a current passport?'

CHAPTER TWO

She preferred to be called Maria rather than Doctor Rogers. I wasn't complaining. She drove me to Stansted in her Merc. I'd got a wheelie-case in the boot and a rucksack with my carry-on bits on the back seat. Travel is not designed for people with a dodgy hand. But this was as comfortable as it could be.

She was certainly not short of money – in fact she was loaded way beyond what she probably earned as a GP. The thing about being in the Force is you soon learn to trust nobody. Fuck it, I didn't even trust myself a lot of the time.

When I asked her about it she just smiled and said 'You're not a cop any longer, Johnny. You're a Private Investigator, and you're working for me. Your job is to keep a watch on my sister and report what she's up to back to me without getting involved. Understood?'

She was right. I was still finding it hard to adjust. I'd gone from first in line for DCI to nobody, more or less overnight. OK, all my mates were sympathetic, but they all knew I'd been a stupid prick to think I could take on a leading member of an organised crime group on my own. Maybe they'd learned a lesson from it, but I wasn't being paid to run classes. The Met had given me a pension, but with a decent pint in London costing six or seven quid I couldn't even drink away my sorrows.

The speed she was driving I wished I'd still had my Warrant Card and a blue light on the top. Still, I knew that any traffic cop who pulled her over was going to get an instant hard-on and jelly knees, so I wasn't that bothered.

'And, Johnny,' she said as we slowed for the drop-off area, 'Don't fall in love with Tina.'

'Would I ever?'

'Oh yes. You think you're falling in love with me. It's just lust. Lust is fine. But love is dangerous, and Tina is dangerous. And eat lots of fish and fruit.'

'I'll try. On both counts.'

'You could get your hand up to ninety percent in a couple of months, but you won't get that just by looking at a menu. Got it?'

'Yes, doctor.'

She pulled into the parking slot and pressed a button. Behind me the boot lid rose majestically. Of course it did — I got the impression that Maria had never been on a package tour in her life. But she did get my case out of the boot and helped me put the rucksack on my back.

*

Stansted. Sigh. Airports are not designed for people to travel, they are designed to sell you things you don't want. You spend half an hour queueing to check your luggage, then another half-hour queueing to have your bag inspected, and then what do they do? Make you walk through endless miles of glossy shops selling perfume. It's all carefully calculated, down to the zigzag tracks that ensure you get a good look at everything on offer. Smellies. Lots of them. During my life as a copper I'd never felt any need to wear perfume. I knew a few who did, but that was usually on their evening off, if they were lucky enough to get one.

Most airports have a solid feel. Not Stansted. The place looked like something from a long-past trade exhibition. The roof was a load of umbrellas stuck together, and the check-in area looked like if you pushed it it'd fall over.

Usually I just walk briskly through and get to the nearest bar. By nearest I mean about half a mile. But on this occasion I did stop on my way and bought a couple of pay-as-you-go phones and plenty of SIM cards. Sure, I'd got my own phone with me, but if you want to live on the margins of the law it's wise to make yourself as hard to trace as possible.

A young woman with too much make-up invited me to sniff something, which I politely declined, and then I turned down a kind offer to buy a raffle ticket for a car. Unless it came with a driver it was fuck-all use to me. I wasn't going to be driving a car any time soon. If ever.

I had two hours to kill before my flight to Corfu, so I sat in the departure area, which they laughably called the Lounge, and had an overpriced pint.

The thing about Ryanair is that Michael O'Leary

doesn't actually rip you off. It's perfectly clear that what you're getting is a bus with wings which will get you from A to B, and not a flying five-star hotel. Some people have never quite caught on to that and they want to fly Club Class for over a thousand miles for twenty quid.

I knew I wasn't going to get anything much to eat on the flight so I decided to get an early lunch. Maria was probably a bloody good doctor, I realised as I ordered curry and chips, because I felt a bit guilty. I'd even passed an eye over the salad offerings on the menu, but that was really a step too far. Why is it we always put off the healthy option until tomorrow?

We all tend to avoid staring at people who are plainly disabled. I guess in a way we wish they would just vanish. I didn't really feel like talking to random strangers, so I kept my hand in clear sight on the table, where it looked like an offcut from a Frankenstein movie. That kept the buggers away.

I got out my Kindle and read a couple of chapters of my science fiction book. I like science fiction because I don't have to worry about it being mostly inaccurate police procedural rules or showing the life of a detective as exciting when it's mostly boring, and after it isn't boring there is a deluge of boring paperwork. So I spent an exciting hour and a half on the surface of Titan worrying about whether my lander had enough fuel to lift off.

Then it was time to make my way to the gate and, as usual, be surprised at how many people were queueing for the plane. I've been to Corfu before, but I don't remember much about it because it was a stag do and we were pissed before we even got on the plane. I've got a faint recollection of doing a tour of bars with shots lined up and very loud music. I don't remember eating anything, and there's a high probability that I didn't.

I'm telling you this so you know I'm not being snobby when I mention the eight women, probably in their early thirties, who were dressed up in bright pink tops and cowboy hats and obviously hellbent on having a great hen party. To say they were loud was putting it mildly. They were averaging about ten shrieks a minute. They could have been on a rollercoaster. I hope the wedding wasn't too soon or the poor bugger who was going to get married to the blonde with the word BRIDE in big letters across the back of her T-shirt was going to be spending most of his honeymoon as a paramedic. Mind you, he was probably paralytic at another holiday spot where he wouldn't make it to the beach. I couldn't criticise, but I hoped the fuck they weren't sitting near me on the plane.

Okay, you guessed. I was sitting in the window seat and then two of them took the seats beside me, while the rest of the party poured themselves into the row in front and the row behind.

The one next to me was a redhead with an award-winning bosom and fake eyelashes. At one time I would have said she had "slag" written all over her but we're not allowed to say that sort of thing any more. She was probably a brain surgeon having a few wild days off — but, somehow, I doubted it but you just can't tell these days.

She was obviously a nervous flyer, because she sat there quiet as a mouse as we pushed back and taxied to the runway. Fine by me.

The plane made satisfactorily loud noises and shoved me back in my seat as we prepared to take off. Are you like me? Do you wonder at this point if there is actually enough tarmac to reach whatever speed is required to get this thing off the ground? No need to worry. The bride-to-be, me, and about a hundred and fifty other people watched the delights of Stansted drop away below us as we climbed into the skies of a very pleasant May afternoon.

My neighbour relaxed, unfortunately. 'What's your name?' she asked.

'What's yours?' I said. I'm a detective. I don't like people asking *me* questions.

'Megan. What you done to your hand?'

The one in the aisle seat leaned forward a bit and said 'I hope he can wank with the other one!'

Plenty of shrieks, and then a loud voice from behind shouted 'Don't worry, mate! She's done more blowjobs than KwikFit!'

I'll say one thing for them – they could scream louder than a jet on its take-off climb. Just visible up ahead in the galley a flight-attendant sighed and shook her head. I sympathised.

I waited until the over-cooked hysteria died

down, raised my voice, and said 'It is a criminal offence to be drunk on an aircraft. Air Navigation Order 2016. Two years in gaol and a five thousand pound fine.'

There was a sudden and long silence. The flight attendant looked up and smiled.

Redhead whispered 'You a copper?'

'Do I look like a copper? Tell you what, Megan – just let me read my book for the next two and a half hours and you'll never need to know.'

It's the little pleasures. Know what I mean?

Call me a miserable bastard. Fair enough. You wouldn't be the first. It's a habit – nobody wants the Old Bill smiling when they nick you, because we're not supposed to enjoy our job, and the Met does everything it can to stop us. Anyway, I got an hour of peace, and a lot of worries about the crew of a spaceship stranded on Saturn's second-largest moon. No, I didn't know that before. Like I didn't know it was bigger than the planet Mercury. Might come in handy in a pub quiz someday.

The flight attendant gave me a big smile and a wink as she dished out a gin & tonic. Nice to know I'd made somebody's job a bit easier.

Megan actually turned out to be quite a nice girl. She saw me fumbling with the ring-pull on my can of tonic water. 'Here. Let me do it,' she said. I was actually concerned that she might break her carefully-manicured fingernail, but she flipped the top and poured me a drink like a pro, which it turned out she was. 'I work in a bar. I have to help a lot of disabled people.'

Ouch.

I put Mister Nasty away for a bit, and gave her a pleasant grin.

'Thanks, Megan.'

If you stripped off a layer of paint and unnecessary accessories, she was pretty.

'Where you going?'

'Corfu, same as you.'

'Nah. When you get there. We're going to Kavos. You bin there? It's fab.'

Somewhere in my much-abused grey matter a small bell rang.

'Maybe. I don't remember much about it. It was a mate's stag do a while ago.'

She leaned across me and pointed out of the window. 'What's all that?'

A vast range of mountains stretched below us. The captain came to my rescue.

'Quick update from the flight deck. We're currently crossing the Dolomites in northern Italy. In about twenty minutes those of you sitting on the left of the plane may get some views of Venice. The weather in Corfu is fine. Twenty-five degrees and sunny. Sit back and enjoy the rest of the flight.'

'D'you ever worry? Like maybe we'll bump into a mountain?'

'There aren't any mountains that go this high. We're about six miles up.'

The girl on the other side of Megan giggled. Megan turned her head towards her and said 'Shut up Tracey, and leave him alone,' which prompted a muted chorus of Oohs. Even I had to smile.

'No fucking class, this lot,' she whispered.

I could have said the same about me and the rest of CID on a night out. Peer pressure is a terrible thing, when you come to think about it. If we'd been in her bar and she'd been working we'd have been commenting loudly on her tits and she'd have been thinking *How bloody long till I can go home?*

Venice appeared as advertised. 'There it is,' I said. She leaned even closer and said 'I've always wanted to go on one of those boats where they sing to you.'

'So do it,' I said.

'Not on me own, stupid.'

I turned my head to look at her. She was very close. I could feel her breath on my cheek. 'Don't worry, Megan,' I said, very quietly. 'I'm sure you'll get there with somebody you like and have a great time.'

She sighed. She'd seen it all before. 'I don't even know your name,' she said.

'Johnny.'

The moment passed. We sat in a kind of amiable silence until the engine sound wound down to idle and all we could see out of the window was blue sea and blue sky.

And then we were flying along the edge of the island; cliffs and hills until the land flattened off and we banked to the left over a strange lake separated from the sea by a long narrow strand of what looked like sand dunes.

'That's weird,' said Megan. She wasn't wrong. 'What is it?'

'I don't know. Could be fresh water or salt water. You could probably walk right along it.'

'Wow!' she said, as the seat-belt sign came on and the cabin crew started the ritual incantation of belts on, seats upright, tables stowed, loose stuff under the seats. 'Can I ask you something?' she added.

'You could try.'

'Are you really a copper, and how'd you do that to your hand?'

'That's two questions. But. I *was* a copper and I'm not now. I got this when I was a copper by being stupid and thinking I was better than I was.'

'What happened?'

'Know what a machete is?'

'No.'

'It's like a cross between a knife and a sword. Used for chopping things. Some toe-rag mistook my hand for sugar cane.'

She paused for a few seconds, sat back a little, and said 'Fuck me. What a bastard!'

No argument from me about that.

'The thing is, Megan, hardly anybody in the police actually gives a shit if you smoke weed or snort a bit of coke. We've all had a few tokes. It's what comes with it. Robbery, child prostitution, people trafficking, violence, blackmail, murder. You can see why I was angry. But that's against the rules, know what I mean?'

'You were a hero.'

'No. I was a complete twat.'

We were flying lower and lower along the coast. Low hills led down to beaches and inlets with handfuls of hotels and little harbours spread out beside the sea. When it seemed like we were below the buildings on our left, suddenly the runway was under us, and we were on Corfu.

She insisted on getting my rucksack down and helped me get it on my back. She shadowed me down the steps from the plane like she was a physio and I was learning to walk again. As we made our way up the ramp to immigration she leaned her head close to mine and whispered.

'I wish I was having a week here with you, and not this lot.'

As things turned out, that might have been a bit less stressful.

CHAPTER THREE

The airport was easy. It'd been done up in tasteful blue, and looked surprisingly modern. Maybe I had been expecting something like a goat-shed. That, it wasn't.

The immigration officer saw me doing my one-and-a-half-handed struggle with the paperwork, said 'Don't bother,' stamped my passport, and waved me through. I hadn't been outside of London since Brexit and it was a bit of a shock to realise we were now aliens in our own continent.

The hen party were cackling away in the baggage claim area. I was reaching for my bag when a slender arm shot forward and grabbed it for me. 'Look after yourself, Johnny. If you're ever in Chelmsford, I'm at Wheeler's Bar. Got it?'

'Yep.'

'Gotta get back.' She kissed me on the cheek and vanished into the crowd.

The taxi was waiting. The driver grabbed my case and led the way past the lines of buses and reps. It was busy. Comings and goings. Cigarette smoke drifted in the warm air, and kids were crying. God, I needed a fag.

Another Merc. I was getting the benefit of German manufacturing today, sitting back in the rear with my rucksack beside me. Corfu town was a pleasant mess of narrow streets and neon signs with strange writing on them. I felt like I ought to be able to read them, and that messed with my head. It was busy. Cars seemed to drive wherever it suited them and then miraculously miss each other. Tourist coaches were pretty good at getting their own way, and everybody seemed to think pedestrians were fair game.

Suddenly we were by the sea and the harbour, where gigantic cruise liners waited for the buses to dump their trippers before they sailed off to who knows where? The narrow road expanded into a dual-carriageway as I felt the unease of driving on the right. Definitely out of my depth here, away from Stokey and Hackney, I gave up wondering whether I should have agreed to this job. I was supposed to be a tourist so I might as well enjoy it.

He was a good talker. Not to me, after a few friendly words, but to someone at the other end of his Bluetooth hands-off mobile. And I mean, like all the way, for three-quarters of an hour. Now and then he had both hands on the wheel, but mostly he was punching the air or holding his chest in anguish. He was like me watching the Arsenal on a Saturday afternoon.

After a long flat strip beside the coast, we turned right and started climbing a mountain range that went right across the horizon. I'd just left behind the last bit of flat land I was going to see for a long time. And the last straight road.

We passed through villages built for the days when a donkey cart was the only form of transport, narrow streets fringed with houses. Every village seemed to have a café of some sort. And a church.

Higher and higher we went, and when we reached the top of the mountain it wasn't the beach I saw, but another range of mountains.

As we coasted down into the valley around a series of hairpin bends the driver lit a cigarette and wound his window down a couple of centimetres. I could have kissed him.

'Alright if I smoke?' I asked.

He carried on talking, driving with one hand, and held the packet between the seats to me.

'Cheers. I thought it was illegal.'

'Fuck the government,' he said, and went back to his Greek conversation. If his was as bad as our bunch of jokers I sympathised entirely.

One thing surprised me as we went around and around and up and down: how green it was. I'd got those pictures in my head of Athens – barren rocks, old stones, parched, dry. But there were trees – dense trees – with terracotta roofs nestling in them. Green trees and reddish-brown tiles. Nothing like the Greece in my mind.

After we crested the next mountains I could see a line of blue sea ahead for a couple of minutes before we were driving through forest. Halfway down there was a huge cleft in the rocks where they'd been blasting out a quarry, and soon after that a yard with a crane and slabs of rock leaning at odd angles.

Where there was a bit of straight road longer than twenty yards the driver floored the accelerator and went past anything in front. Come to think of it, he did that on the bends as well.

We flashed passed a shop with a big sign saying "Olive Wood" in English, and soon after he slowed as we entered a big village.

'*Arillas*,' he said. 'Soon there.'

He turned right just past a place with chairs and tables outside and big pictures of ice-cream. That's when I realised I was hungry. Up another hill, down a twisting road with flowering shrubs on the side, and then there was a sign which read *Agios Stefanos*. Looked like we were there.

We went passed a bar which called itself *3 Ws.* I found out later that it stood for World Wide Web and it used to be an Internet café before everybody had a flashy phone in their pocket, or more likely their hand.

The car slowed to halt outside a three-storey building set back from the road. The driver cancelled his mobile call, heaved his considerable bulk out of the door as the boot opened behind me. I grabbed my rucksack and climbed awkwardly out of the car. I took sixty-five euros our of my wallet and gave it to him – then added another ten. He smiled, said something that sounded like "Ever his toe" and then added 'Thank you.'

He beat me to the wheelie case in the boot and began dragging it across the road.

Artemis Apartments was tastefully inscribed on

a pale blue board on the wall. A wide flight of steps led up to just above eye-level, and as I climbed it I got my first view of the garden. There was a big swimming pool with sun-beds and parasols around it. Various people were stretched out in the May sunshine, some reading, some just grilling. The pool was blue and calm, with a small bar at the bottom of the main building.

The upper two levels of *Artemis* consisted of two rows of six balconies, one or two with towels hanging over. There was a big satellite dish, and on the top of the building a blue and white Greek flag stirred lethargically.

The driver elbowed the glass door open and held if for me to go in. He parked my bag beside a long reception counter and shouted something in Greek. Then he turned and smiled. 'Thanks, mate,' I said as he walked away. Nice bloke. The first of many.

She walked in through a side-door. Fuck me! Maria! Only not quite. Or was that just that her dark hair was tied back?

You get used to staring at faces in CID. Is that one on a CCTV camera the one you're looking for? Is that rat-bitten mess the missing woman? Do I know that face?

Could Maria seriously have forgotten to tell me she had a twin? Bloody doctors always tell you the minimum.

'You must be Mr Almond.'
'Got it in one.'

'I'm Tina. You're in room seven on the second floor. Let me show you.'

She grabbed my rucksack before I could pick it up, and led the way to the stairs. I followed, case in my left hand.

'Have you been to *Agios Stefanos* before?'

'Never.'

'Well- You'll find most people here have been coming for twenty or thirty years. Hope you enjoy it.'

'I'll do my best.'

She opened my room door and showed me how to put the fob into a slot to turn on the electrics. Then a broad, professional smile. 'Are you John or Johnny?'

'Usually Johnny – but I answer to John. Don't like Johnno much.'

'Okay, Johnny. Anything else you need?'

'A beer and something to eat would be good.'

'Turn left out of the front and you're in the middle of the village. Beer and food everywhere. If you need me, just shout.'

'Will do, Tina.'

'There's a little map in the pack on the side there. It's not hard. The road we're on runs down the valley to the sea, then turns left to the harbour. A hundred yards or so from here as you walk towards the sea another road goes to the right and then up a steep hill. Most bars and eating places are on that road. Okay?'

She went out, closing the door behind her.

I looked around. The room was huge. Two single beds had been put together to make a kind of double. There were brown wood built-in wardrobes, a dining table and three chairs, a sofa, a flat-screen telly on the wall, a desk unit, a kitchen area with a fridge and an electric hob with two black rings on a unit.

The bathroom had a modern glass-walled shower, bog and handbasin. I took a leak and thought 'This is pretty nice.'

At the far end of the room were some glass doors leading onto a big balcony with a round white plastic table and some chairs. We were in a green valley between hills. In the distance back up the valley, a plume of steam or smoke rose from some plant. Otherwise, the only thing moving was a fat geezer with secondary sunburn who was floating around in the pool.

It was quiet. I stuck my bag on the bed beside the towels, which were carefully arranged into bows, dug some shorts out, dropped my sweaty long-sleeved shirt on the floor, pulled a T-shirt over my head, took my socks off and put my trainers back on.

I can use my right hand, but it hurts like fuck and I can't do anything delicate. It's not a hand – it's a bunch of bananas with a needle stuck in it. Word of advice: don't try to be a hero – go in mob-handed and tooled-up. No bloody wonder my mates called me "Nutcase" Almond.

First rule of sleuthing, police or private, is get

to know the environment. I was supposed to see what Tina was up to and who she was up to it with. Piece of cake, here. Tourists have bugger all else to do but wander about slowly looking at people and places. Try that in Stokey and alarm bells would ring and you'd be on a dozen mobile phone cameras and uploaded before you'd got to the end of Church Street.

They were all still prone around the pool as I walked out of the building and down the steps to the road. I turned left towards the village. I passed a tennis court on my right, and on my left the hill rose steeply. I passed a smart taverna. Under the sign which read *Vaso &Yianni* people were lounging about finishing their lunch, and the smell of grilling and herbs turned my hunger into an instant ache.

About forty yards on I came to the main T-junction. There was a holiday apartment block on the right, where the second road went down a gentle slope, and then climbed up into the distance. Just a little way further on my left was exactly what I was looking for – a café called *Tasty Corner*, raised about five feet above road level with a perfect view of the junction and up the opposite street. Simple tables and chairs, mostly in the open air with a canopy. Nothing fancy. Just the job.

I chose a table with a good view. Two old men were drinking small cups of coffee and talking loudly in Greek. The menu was short and to the point. The owner came over, and I ordered a chicken kebab, chips and a beer, lit a fag, and sat back to watch my surroundings.

There wasn't much going on. A moped came down the sloping road opposite at high speed, its engine whining, slowed a tiny amount and turned along the road to my left. The rider wasn't wearing a helmet.

A frosted glass arrived on my table, and a bottle with a green label shortly after. My first, but not my last, bottle of "Mythos." There was a large bar opposite, with a shaded area under a permanent canopy, and other tables with parasols. Six or seven people were relaxing in comfy-looking chairs with a glass of something on the low tables in front of them.

Being under-cover here obviously meant spending a lot of time sitting around drinking. That was going to be tough.

What was not tough was the kebab. It was juicy, with tender lumps of grilled chicken. I didn't even have to ask for ketchup. They obviously knew their customers. It was perfect for me. I could just use a fork in my left hand, and I could manage to hoist the beer in my right.

I sent a text to Maria. "Arrived. Will begin surveillance shortly. Is Tina your twin?"

To be honest, I was knackered. Long day. The food and the beer were having their inevitable impact. I wandered back up the road feeling like I might crash out for a couple of hours.

CHAPTER FOUR

Tina was behind the pool bar when I got back. Mr Sunburn was on a bar stool. His belly was hanging down over his shorts and he looked like an overweight lobster gleaming with sweat.

'Been to the beach?' she asked.

'Nope. I only made it as far as *Tasty Corner*.'

'Great little place, that,' Mr Sunburn said. Northern accent.

Tina said 'Plenty of time. What can I get you?'

'Can I have a Mythos?' Except I pronounced it "M-eye-those."

'Course you can,' she said, smiling. 'It's said like "MEE-thoss." Glass?'

I nodded, and said 'Please.'

'First time here?' Mr Sunburn asked.

'Afraid so.'

'You'll be back. We've been coming to San Stef for twenty-seven years, regular as clockwork. Tenerife in't winter, San Stef in't summer.' He stuck his hand out and said 'Alan.'

I put my left hand forward. He looked puzzled for a minute, then saw the scars across my right hand.

'Johnny,' I said.

Tina pushed a glass and a bottle across the bar. 'On me,' she said.

'Now then,' Alan said, puffing up with fake indignation. 'You've never given me a beer!'

'You've never deserved one. Excuse me. Things to do.' She walked away into the building.

I didn't reckon that Alan was going to be a bosom pal, but he could be useful. I desperately needed some local knowledge if I was going to get anywhere.

'Known Tina a long time?' I asked, pouring some beer into his glass and mine.

'Yes, pal. Eight years or so, give and take. Nice lass. She's had a tough time, though.'

'Why's that?'

'Her husband, Spiros. Typical Greek bloke, know what I mean? Left her for a Swedish rep. Not that I've got anything against the Greeks, of course.'

I laughed. 'He was either blind, or the Swedish rep must have been a pretty fantastic looker.'

'I wouldn't kick either of them out of bed! Know what I mean?'

'Lucky bastard.'

He took a good gulp of beer. 'Apparently her grandfather came from round here. Went to England and made a lot of money with dodgy rentals. Bit of a Rachman, I reckon. But you'd be too young to know about him.'

'Slum landlord. Nineteen-sixties in London. So, she's got Greek blood.'

There was a was a shout from down the pool. Alan raised his eyebrows and said 'Bugger it. That's my better half. Anything you want to know, just ask, Johnny.'

He prised himself off the stool and walked slowly away. I sat for a while sipping my beer, thinking about the fact that I was as out of my depth as a gerbil in the deep end of the pool a few yards from me.

While I finished the Mythos, I started joining the dots. Two women – well-spoken – probably private school – with Greek family connections right here. The grandfather into possibly dubious property rental. You've don't have to be in the Met for long to know that property and construction go hand in hand with crime. At the high end it's overseas money and offshore tax evasion, corrupt contracting, corner-cutting developers. At the low end it's bullying, violence, forced prostitution, exploitation.

And Tina wasn't running a nice GP Practice in North London. She was back here, where the old man came from. At which point she emerged from the office or whatever was behind that door. She didn't look happy until she saw me watching her, and the smiled that professional smile that all front-facing people can turn on like a light-bulb.

'Another beer?'

'Thanks, Tina. I'm fine. Might have a kip.'

'Why not? You're on holiday.'

I did my not very good impression of her well-honed smile. 'It's really nice, this place. Been working here long?'

'Well – I don't exactly *work* here. I own it. Actually, I half own it.'

'Wow. Who's got the other half?'

Ease off, Johnny. You're not in an interview room at the Stoke Newington nick. But she wasn't fazed.

'It's a family thing. Everything in this village is a family thing. What happened?' She pointed to my left hand. Clever – she'd answered and diverted the topic, just like I would have done.

'Let's just say I had an accident. It's a nuisance, but don't worry - I'm not going to die on you.'

Her eyes were very dark brown – almost black, and I realised that her olive skin wasn't just suntan but the bit of Greek in her.

'Please don't,' she said. 'It causes a lot of paper-work.'

'I'm not being rude, but you don't sound like you come from round here.'

'I was born in London. If you count Richmond as London. Third generation Greek. You?'

'Oh – Islington. The poor bit, before it came out all tapas bars and stupidly expensive shops.'

'That's north London, isn't it?'

I didn't say it, but I was *thinking Oh, come on, Tina! Your sister's a doctor in Stokey. You know bloody well where Islington is. So why pretend?*

'Sure is,' I said. 'I'm off for a kip. Thanks for the beer.'

'You're very welcome, Johnny.' Big smile, and we went our separate ways.

I went up to my room, stripped off, stretched out on the bed and pulled the sheet over me. I used the burner phone to call Tariq at Stoke Newington nick. Tariq was a good bloke. I'd worked with him a lot and I took his side when there was a rash of Paki jokes in the canteen. We agreed about a lot of things – mainly that the world was full of idiots and you might as well ignore them and get on with the job. He was a token Muslim – never went to the mosque, liked a drink and a smoke, reckoned it was pointless getting married when there was an endless supply of the necessary in and around the nick.

The thing is, Tariq understood the difference between information and useful information. You can get blinded by information. Finding out that a suspect wears size eleven shoes is only useful if you have a footprint at a crime scene.

He answered his mobile straightaway, and after the usual banter I told him the info I wanted. Strictly illegal, of course, but Tariq was smart enough to construct a plausible cover-story for anything. Plus the fact that senior officers were shit-scared of facing accusations of racism and bent over backwards to give him the benefit.

I dozed off for an hour, had a long shower with warm water, and made myself a cup of tea with one of the teabags I'd brought with me at Maria's suggestion. There was a carton of milk in the fridge and some sugar in the cupboard. Mental note – get some biscuits.

The WiFi signal was good when I fired up the laptop and typed in the password that was in a folder on the table. Mail from Tariq.

"Hi you old tosser. Bottle of Scotch (not Greek) for this.

"Dr Maria Gregory. Born Maria Alexaki. 42 years. Has a twin - Katerina. Father Spiros Alexakis owns a construction company. Grandfather also Spiros died in prison with suspected foul play after conviction for racketeering and violence in slum properties in Southall. Maria divorced English husband Steven Gregory two years ago on grounds of adultery. Father investigated by Fraud Squad but insufficient evidence. Dr G senior partner in medical practice in Clissold Park. No dirt found. Any more is two bottles. Deal?"

I replied 'Fucking extortion but yes. Cheers mate. See you when I get back.'

I shut the laptop down and got dressed. Time for a walkabout.

There was no sign of Alan or Tina as I left Artemis and headed into the village. There were plenty of people about. It was seven-thirty. Most of the women had put dresses on and the men seemed to divide between shorts and long trousers or jeans. The air was full of the scent of aftershave and perfume, mixed with wafts of barbecuing lamb and herbs.

I headed straight down the road towards the beach. I passed the T-junction and carried on past *Tasty Corner* and its bar called *El Greco*. Next was a big apartment complex, bar and taverna called *The Little Prince*, with some shops opposite. Then I came to a smart outdoor coffee bar and a shop selling newspapers, hats, blow-up rubber rings, towels and other useful holiday stuff. There was a sign saying "Shops within a shop."

On the right side was an open space where there were cars parked and quad-bikes parked, and beyond that big stands of bamboo. The road snaked up a slope and curved to the left and then to the right. The hills rose steeply to the left. I passed a smart-looking eatery called *Olympia*, raised well up from the road, and then I crested the slope and faced downhill towards the sun – now dropping as sunset approached.

Don't worry – this is not a travel brochure. I needed to get the place into my head, and I'm just telling it as I saw it. Okay?

This was not an old place. It was obviously fairly modern. But the concrete buildings had loads of flowering shrubs and palm trees to soften the edges. There were flowers everywhere – particularly red and yellow.

Going down the slope there was an unfinished building on the right with skeletal concrete pillars and dangerous-looking stairs with no handrails. A few yards further and there was a shop selling olive-wood knick-knacks, and a juice bar near a junction. A small road went at a steep angle up the hill to the left.

Ahead, the road curved away to the left past a sign saying "Port" and another small road carried on down past a little supermarket, gift shop, ATM. There was a building on the corner with big

pictures of trips and scenery – *San Stefano Travel*.
There was sand drifting across the road. I crossed
over and headed down the slope between the
supermarket and the travel agent. On my right was
a small, smart apartment building.

Twenty-five yards on and I was on the beach.
Jesus – it went on as far as the eye could see. It
was a vast reach of sand. I was beside a stream
which emerged from the bamboo and ended in
some shallow sandy ponds. There were a few cars
and quad-bikes parked on my left, and then some
beach-side tavernas with brollies and sunbeds. On
the other side of the stream the beach vanished up
to the horizon, and I could see more sunbeds and
bars.

I walked ahead past a little rickety bridge over
the stream and came to the edge of the sea, which
lapped gently onto a sandy shore fringed with
dark, fine strands of seaweed. Ripples came in
from way out and didn't so much break as give up
with a gentle splosh when they reached the shore.

Out to sea there were islands, low on the horizon, and in the distance to the right a hazy line of
mountains, which I later learned were Albania. No
bloody wonder people came back.

By this time the sun was low to the left, with a
line of rippling gold across the sea towards me. I
watched it for a while, thinking that I wasn't going
to have much trouble posing as a tourist here.

CHAPTER FIVE

The sun set over one of the islands. When it disappeared, the sky lit up with a huge show of colours: reds and purples, and some great splashes of green. I realised then that this village wasn't beautiful, but it had front-row seats in a great natural theatre of sea and light. Don't start on about how would I know that kind of thing – I might be just a damaged plod to you, but I did do A Level English back in the day before I ended up dealing with low-life as a day-job. Rule number two of being a detective: things are never quite what they seem. I kind of fell into being a copper, and when I fell out of being a copper I kind of fell into what I was doing now.

Maybe I'd be better off chucking it in and getting a job in one of the cafés along the beach.

I walked back up the way I'd come, and went into the paper shop to buy some fags. Turns out it was owned by two sisters. I was amazed how cheap the cigarettes were – just over three quid a packet as opposed to ten in the UK. How many smokers would have voted for Brexit if they'd known this was coming?

The Little Prince looked lively. It was a big building, three storeys, and the lower section had a big wooden roof covering lots of tables. Almost all full. There was a buzz of chatter, and a waiter was carrying something letting off clouds of steam.

As I walked up the steps from the road I could see the restaurant was on two levels, with tables on an upper section and big doors that led inside. I reached the top and a woman, not very tall with dark hair and big dark shrewd eyes, came across from the till.

'Just one? She asked.

''Fraid so. Is that okay?'

'Of course.'

She led me to a table near the end of the top section and pulled a chair out for me.

'Drink?'

The thing is, I like a beer with a curry, but in the evening, somehow, I prefer a drop of plonk. I used to get the piss taken when I went out with CID but I just told them to fuck off. That all ended when we got a new DCI – woman called Laura Meadows. Whenever she was there we shared a bottle of red and nobody said a bloody word. Of course, there were rumours we were having it off, but we definitely weren't.

I liked Laura. She was good. Some of the blokes had it against her because she was a woman, but she was smart and on the ball. Boy was she tough. She came to see me in hospital. No flowers, no grapes – just 'You're a total dickhead, Johnny. Get the fuck better. I need you.' But then she smiled, bent over my bed and kissed the top of my head. 'You can still be the best.' She opened my bedside cabinet, took a bottle of Beaujolais and a glass out of her big bag and put them inside.

'I'm sure you'll be able to charm some little nurse into pouring it for you,' With that, she just turned and left.

I thought for a few seconds while the woman with dark hair looked at me expectantly.

'Can I have a glass of red wine?'

'Just a glass, or a carafe? It's cheaper if you want more than one.'

'That sounds good.'

'Litre or half litre?'

They sure as hell didn't do things small here. But. I was supposed to be working.

'Half, please.'

She nodded and said something in Greek to the slender young man with a wide toothy smile who was putting a basket of bread and some cutlery on the table.

I leaned back in my chair and lit a cigarette. I'd already clocked the ashtray on the table, so I reckoned that was fine, and I'd already noticed a good-looking blonde two tables along puffing on a fag. She was probably in her early forties, sitting with a man with dark hair and a longish nose, maybe her husband. They had a big glass jug of white wine on the table. Looking around, everybody seemed relaxed and cheerful. I'd better fit in.

The waiters all wore black and white. Black trousers and white tops or T-shirts.

Mr Smile came back with a smaller glass jug of red wine and poured some into my glass. I thanked him and he said '*Parakolo.* How are you doing?'

'Pretty good. What's your name?'

'Thanassis. Dimitris will take your order when you're ready.' He pointed to a tall man with greying hair who was chatting to the blonde and her husband. I got the impression they were old buddies.

The waiter smiled again and went away. I studied the menu. This is always the point where I get a pain in my right hand, because I could have murdered a steak, but by now I was used to the idea of fork food above all else. You can switch a computer mouse to be left-handed, but there's no magic button to make your left hand as good as your right. Bummer. It'd be a big day for me if I could hack my way through a rump with mushroom and chips.

Dimitris was a pro – no doubt about that. He was constantly looking around while he talked and laughed with the others. The second I put the menu down he came over with a tablet for the order and said 'Have you decided?'

'I need a bit of help. Something that doesn't need cutting up.'

His eyes flicked over my scars and he nodded. 'How about moussaka?'

'What's that?'

'Greek shepherd's pie. Lamb mince, aubergine, cinnamon, bechamel topping. My grandmother's recipe. It's good. Best in the village.'

'How can I refuse?'

He nodded. 'Good choice. Chips or roast potatoes?'

'Roast.' He tapped the tablet. 'Starter?'

'Surprise me.'

What came was yoghurt totally loaded with garlic and triangles of pitta bread to scoop it up with. The garlic was fiery on my tongue, but it sure worked on my appetite. The moussaka was rich with cinnamon and the bechamel topping had been browned under the grill.

The lights went down and the music went from quiet to loud. Another waiter came in with a wooden table and chair and smacked them down. Thanassis had tied a red bandana round his waist and he danced. Usually I find blokes dancing a bit embarrassing and to be honest where I come from it's more likely to be girls twined round poles, but he was good. Dimitris had a couple of plastic bottles with some liquid in and he sprayed stuff all over the table and the chair on the top of it. Flick of a lighter and the whole lot burst into yellow and blue flames. Thanassis danced forward and picked the table up in his teeth and carried on dancing. Dimitris squirted more liquid on. Round and round went waiter, table and flames. People were standing and taking pictures on their phones. On the last beat of the music, perfectly timed, Thanassis dropped the table and came to attention. There was lots of applause. The lights came back up.

I'd nearly finished the moussaka when Dimitris came over to see how I was doing. He noticed that the wine had nearly all gone, walked away quickly and came back with another jug. 'On the house,' he said, and filled my glass. The taverna was quieter, and nobody new was coming in. He sat down at my table and lit a cigarette. Then he shouted something incomprehensible to Thanassis and turned to me.

'First time here?' he asked. I'd noticed that everywhere you went in this village they asked you if you'd been before, unless you arrived with your luggage for the umpteenth time, in which case you got hugged.

I nodded. 'Arrived today.' Thanassis brought a glass of white wine over and gave it to Dimitris, who raised it and said 'Yiamass! Cheers!'

We clinked glasses. 'I'm Dimitris,' he said. He pointed to the woman with the big eyes and said 'That's my wife, Pipina. Anything you want, just ask.'

Perfect technique. If you want to find out somebody's name, introduce yourself. They will feel like they have to respond. In polite society, of course. On the backstreets of Hackney our lot would just ask for your name and address and squeeze you against the squad car until you replied. Well, if you were black, that is.

'Johnny,' I said.

'Welcome, Johnny. Where are you staying?'

'Up the road at *Artemis*.'

He nodded. There was something in his eyes I couldn't quite get. Was it disapproval? I'd have to work on that.

He picked up my wine jug and said 'Come and

meet Andy and Gill.' He led the way to the table where the good-looking blonde and her fella were sitting.

They were good company. He was from the Midlands – she was from Cumbria. Andy and Gill. Been here for donkeys' years, and even sometimes jetted over for a long weekend. They reckoned it was the most relaxing place they'd ever found, and who was I to argue? It was two in the morning when I got back to *Artemis*, climbed under my sheet and slept until nine in the morning.

I had a cup of tea and went for a run into the village and up the road that branched to the right near *Tasty Corner*. Soon after I turned right I could smell baking bread. The bakery was up some steps. Outside, a man wearing a floury apron and a young woman were loading trays of loaves into a small white van. Instant hunger, but I carried on up the road, which was lined with shops, bars and eateries: *Bar38, Zorba's, Elizabeth's, Condor, Silver Moon.* There were supermarkets and scooter and bike rentals, people washing the pavement outside their places, delivery vans stocking the village for a new day. This was obviously the main drag, and it got steeper the further I went. Just above a firmly-closed restaurant called *Sunset* the buildings thinned out and the road carried on up the hill. I wasn't training for a bloody marathon, so I turned back, ran down the hill to near the junction and went into the bakery. There were racks of long crispy loaves and glass-fronted cabinets with savoury and sweet pastry events. I bought a loaf and some apple pie – which cost next to nothing – and then bought more milk and yoghurt and honey in the little supermarket next door.

When I need to think, I go for a walk or a run, and what I had been thinking was what a tosser I was. This was not a job for me. I had no chance here. I was stuffed.

Talking to Andy and Gill had clued me up a lot. This village was a big family operation – well, two families, a bit like Romeo and Juliet although they'd eased back a bit on the violence because they'd all intermarried. Most of them lived up the hill where I'd been running, in an old village. Each family had its own church, as though God was running a kind of *holier than thou* football league. Until forty years ago this place was just a small fishing harbour. Then there were a couple of tavernas and a hotel in a part of the village I hadn't been to.

One by one, new apartment blocks and tavernas opened up as tourism went from an adventurous few to just about everybody. There wasn't a lot of building land, because this was a valley, but the Greeks are good at slotting stuff into what space was available. There was a meeting early each year when the families decided on prices for beer and food. They kept the prices low, and got the attention of some big tour operators like Thomas Cook and Thomson.

Over the hill to the south, the next village, *Ar-*

illas, was popular with the Germans, but here was the kingdom of the Brits. It wasn't a poncy posh place with over-priced shops catering for those with a lot of disposable income, but it wasn't a burger-joint. It didn't have a disco. Apparently, they left all that to a bigger village a few miles away. It was too far from the airport to attract the stag and hen party "let's get pissed at all costs" crowd. What they had created was a carefully-crafted Greek experience with a great beach and food subtly adjusted to suit ordinary hard-working or retired people who wanted some sun and a relaxed time. Bad behaviour was out of order. There were no shot-drinking competitions. The excessively arse-holed got chucked out of bars.

All of which was good news for me as a tourist, but bad news as a detective. At the first sign of me being nosy they'd close ranks in an instant, just like the ethnic communities in London. All I could do was stay within the bounds of acceptable curiosity, keep my eyes open, and hope I got lucky.

What I needed was somebody who was from here but not from here, if you see what I mean.

I went back to my room and sat on the balcony eating my (delicious) apple pie with some yoghurt and honey, looking out over the pool. The sun was well up by now and it was time to plan my next moves. Alan and his Mrs were already stretched out on sunbeds by the pool. A couple of other people were spreading towels out and adjusting the sunshades.

I switched on the laptop, did a few searches, and made a phone call, using a burner. Then I slung some swimming shorts into a light bag with a towel and went to the beach.

CHAPTER SIX

I crossed a little bridge over the stream and walked to where there were loads of sunbeds widely-spaced in ranks. The sand was firm. I wandered to the edge of the sea, which was calm and still, apart from some little ripples right at the edge, skirting around a small child sitting in a water-filled hole he'd dug in the beach. There was a red plastic bucket and spade beside him and he splashed happily, civil engineering accomplished, taking it easy. Well done, mate. You've earned it. Wish I had.

Jesus, this beach was big. I passed a floating platform with a parachute spread out on it and a motor-boat parked nearby. There were a few people walking about in the sea, and a couple playing bat and ball beside the water.

The sun was higher and it had a bit of power in it. I had a sudden simultaneous desire for a swim and a beer. I settled for a bed on the strip in front of a bar with a big sign reading *Havana*, paid eight euros, struggled into my swimmies under my towel and headed for the deep blue sea.

Or not, as it turned out. You could walk for fifty yards here and still be only up to your waist. It was deceptive – sandbars meant you'd get a deeper bit and then a shallower bit. I went through the threshold where the sea finally hits your balls and makes you feel you've been kicked in the goollies by a snowman; I poured cool water over the back of my neck like my dad had taught me to do at Southend, and finally launched myself forward.

I hadn't tried swimming since I'd been hacked by a Hackney drug baron. It's fucking hard to swim with one hand. One-handed crawl? Forget it. Breast stroke? Great for going around in circles. I settled for turning on my back and kicking my legs, although that way the sun was in my eyes, and the problem was that when I squeezed them shut I got images of a glass full of beer. I'm old enough to know that if I'd been sitting with a beer and not gone in the sea I'd be seeing visions of being in the water. Why are we like that?

Eventually I waded back to shore. My legs were aching. You could get fit here just getting out to where the water was above your waist and back, let alone swimming.

The guy who ran *Havana Bar* was energetic and friendly. He was another Spiros. Dimitris told me last night that just about every first-born son was called Spiros after their patron saint, who wasn't called Spiros. No wonder I felt totally out of my depth apart from in the sea. But here I was, sitting in the shade of a canopy, drinking a Mythos and munching my way through a Caesar Salad when I really should have been following Tina around with a telephoto lens seeing what she was up to. It was only Day One, FFS, and I had to establish my cover, so I was working hard at being a tourist.

Awful.

My phone pinged: text message.

Right. I was about to blow a lot of my fee and expenses, but I didn't have much choice. That's the way it goes. What I spent was tax-deductible, so I was diverting cash I wouldn't have got anyway to the Greek economy. Fair enough. Judging from last night's chat it seemed the Greeks were about as keen on paying taxes as a duck was on orange sauce. What I liked about the text was the detail: the bus I should get, where I should get off, where I should go, who I should look for, what I should bring. No messing. I sent back "Okay. See you there."

Another beer? Why not?

Then I walked back down to the beach and turned right along the sand. The cliffs were getting steeper on my right, and the sea with its small waves on my left. There was a patch of sunbeds, a boat hire place with a Greek flag, and then the sunbeds thinned out.

Another fifty yards and I saw some people skinny-dipping, and then a couple near the cliffs stretched out naked on towels. One of the men in the sea called out something in German. That figured. They love taking their clothes off and getting the sun on Herr Dick and, from what I could see, Fraulein Shave-It-Off. I don't give a shit if people want to wave it about, although I've never seen the point myself. But it did seem a bit like making a statement. Was I morally lacking for keeping my trunks on?

The cliffs got taller and the beach got narrower. There was grey debris from cliff-falls piled at the bottom of the steep rock-faces. A gentle breeze blew in from the sea, which had driftwood and fragments of nets bobbing along the edge. There was nobody here – just me and the cliffs and the sea. I was in another world. I wandered along, splashing through the warm shallows, feeling better than I had for a long time. My right hand was not hurting so much and I was full of food and friendliness.

My appointment for the next day made me feel as though I'd done something for the cause. Truth to tell, this was the most relaxed I'd felt since the day of my "accident." You can't relax in hospital. If you actually manage to doze off they wake you up to test something or give you pills or tell you that you really should drink more water or eat more of the tasteless cold food or prod you where it hurt most. The nurses were all tired and stressed-out. The doctors were a bit full of themselves, and the consultants trailed more acolytes around than the Queen of Sheba; they had this habit of standing at the end of your bed with their back to you addressing the nurses and students whilst totally ignoring or inviting any input from you. And the students – they were a mixture of arrogance and terror. I felt sorry for them on the whole because they obviously had to try to seem intelligent at the same time as not appearing to be more intelligent than the consultant. Bit like an interview with a senior police officer. One of them hung back after the consultant had started moving away and asked if he could look at my penis.

'I've got a serious machete wound in my hand and you want to examine my dick? Why?'

'Just a theory I have.'

'Listen. I'm not denying there's a historical relationship between the hand and the todger, but really I think you'd be better off listening to Mr Ahmed, because he may be a bit arrogant, but he stitched my ligaments and nerves together and he has never shown any interest in my dick. Got it?'

In the unlikely event you're at all interested in my dick, I can tell you that it's probably about average size. One of my girlfriends once said to me it was a perfect fit and her previous fella had been so big it hurt. Was that a compliment?

Talking of big – they really like feeding you in this village. They do not do small. That evening I went on the main strip and ate at *Zorbas* – lamb and apricots in a pot, with rice, and a big jug of vino or whatever they called it here. Can't remember. Anyway, two guys danced like you wouldn't believe – twisting, turning, fast footwork, perfectly together. This was on another level. And a fiery table with a pretty girl doing a belly-dance on top. Lifting a burning table in the teeth? Oh yes.

Back home your average waiter looked exhausted if they had to carry extra chips out with your steak; here they did all that AND danced.

Despite the obvious fact that the Gooners are the greatest football team in the galaxy, I doubt if any of them could have survived a few nights of this. And it was only May now and the evening was a bit chilly. Could they manage this in August when it went up to forty? I remembered some prick in the Stokey nick talking about fat Greeks. So far, I hadn't seen any, but there was no shortage of wobbling Brits. These guys were fit, lean and strong, and I was impressed, so I stopped thinking that men dancing was boys in tutus. Could they all do this?

The one who was obviously the head honcho came around seeing if everybody was okay, so I asked him.

'Yes,' he said. 'We start when we're two or three years old.'

He introduced himself. His name was Pavlos.

'What about the girls?'

'Sure. We like to dance. See my wife in there?' He pointed to a stunning woman standing behind the bar in the main building. 'She's a great dancer.'

'So are you and the other guy.'

'That's Vassilis. He's very popular with the older ladies.'

Vassilis heard his name and smiled at me with a broad cheeky grin.

The young woman who'd been belly-dancing had changed back into sensible clothes. She brought me a plate of water-melon and a small glass of what turned out to be a sort of plum brandy. I remembered my fifth-form history teacher telling us how Alexander the Great's armies conquered the known world, and I realised how they did it. They filled their enemies with food and booze and danced around them.

I went to bed hoping that I was going to get one of them on my side tomorrow. But I sure as hell wasn't sure.

CHAPTER SEVEN

After a trip to the bakery and supermarket I had a breakfast of tea, toast and honey, decided my fawn chinos and blue T-shirt would be better than shorts, and headed down to get the ten o'clock bus to Sidari. I waited in the shade of the taverna and apartments on the corner – *Barras* it was called – and eyed the Sunday roast menu chalked on a board on the wall. The bus-stop was a faded green metal affair with an equally faded timetable behind cracked glass. My rucksack, now empty, was on my left shoulder.

There's a very British idea that only in Germany do trains run on time, and anywhere in the Mediterranean the buses were always late, so I was a bit surprised when a green single-decker rounded the corner from the direction of *Little Prince*, smack on time. A couple of tourists and an old woman in black climbed up the stairs before me.

There was actually a conductor. I hadn't seen one of those for a long time. I used my Oyster card on the 73 in Stoke Newington, and the tube. This was the kingdom of cash. It was ridiculously cheap. I hadn't mastered euro coins yet, so the conductor picked a couple out of my outstretched change and gave me a ticket. We went up the hill, past *Zorba*'s and *Sunset*, and then up and up, curving to the left and the right, past a couple of blocks with swimming pools. It was steep.

Outside a modern building called *Romanza* we picked up a young couple, and climbed even further. I had a great view of the bay and the sea, and at last we turned right and the road levelled off for a bit, until we climbed another hill and were suddenly in a village of old houses and narrow streets. After all the ups we started steeply down. The village was built on a hillside. The old woman got off the bus by a village square below the road level.

I consulted my instructions. This was *Avliotes*, where most of the owners and workers in *Agios Stefanos* lived. Dimitris had told me they always built villages high up, to get the cool breeze and avoid the pirates. That made sense: the pirates would have been totally knackered if they'd had to climb the hill to get here.

Out of the village we went down and the road flattened out; it wasn't long before we came to the outskirts of a new village. Houses and small blocks, all with orange-red pantile roofs, a few tavernas advertising pizza and kebabs, a field with some horses, a couple of dogs stretched out by the roadside.

Then we were going through the centre of *Sidari*. It was a wide, flat coastal plain, a promenade, a one-way road system, and hundreds of small apartment blocks. We passed a Chinese restaurant with a bridge over a fake stream, and went around an open space with some construction going on. That was my cue from my instructions and I got up, hanging on with one hand, and signalled to the conductor. He nodded.

We stopped near a busy crossroad and I climbed down, along with a few others, and walked down towards the sea, which I could glimpse between buildings. At the crossroads, what looked like the main drag went to the left and what I assumed was the road out of town went to the right. It was nothing like the village I'd come from – there were burger bars and happy hour signs, and I saw a young woman in hot-pants eating candy floss. Fuck me, I thought – this is Clacton on a hot day, if such a thing is possible.

Don't get me wrong. I'm not a snob. I'm as ordinary as it comes, but maybe I'm a bit choosy. Something that's simple and honest is fine by me, but this looked like a tacky tourist machine with no soul.

It was hard work crossing the road. The drivers here didn't take prisoners, and it was busy. The bus turned right round an impossible right-angle, with about half an inch to spare on either side. Cars backed up and pulled in, because this guy was giving way to nobody. I made it to the other side and walked towards the beach.

There it was: a little taverna and coffee place on the left, more or less hidden unless you came past. Nice light-yellow Italian-style parasols shaded the tables around the open-air area and bright red flowers grew from wooden boxes. A few people were scattered round drinking coffee or an early beer and bouzoukis played quietly in the background.

Private Investigator Sophia Papadopoulou was sitting alone at one of the tables reading a book. I took the chance to get a good look at her before I sat down: mid-fifties, neatly-trimmed black wavy hair, narrow straight nose, sun-glasses pushed up onto the top of her head, black trousers and a white short-sleeved blouse. Was it possible, I wondered, to get trousers any other colour than black here?

I walked over.

'Sophia,' I said.

She smiled: very white American-style teeth. 'Seen enough?' She gestured to a chair at the table, and I sat down. 'You could work on your surveillance skills. How's your hand doing?'

Okay. This was going to be a bit of a contest. I was up for that. After a few years in the Force you can spot a woman copper a mile away.

'No and fine,' I said. 'I thought I was hiring you and not the other way around.'

'I'm choosy about my clients. John Peter Almond, ex-CID, maybe a hero, maybe an idiot, turns up on this island and makes some – unusual – requests. The question is – do I trust him?'

She leaned back. She was slim, but her blouse stretched over her breasts, which were surprisingly big.

'Done some research, then.'

'Of course. Do you just take on any case because it walks in through the door? Jealous husband –

no problem. Jealous wife – no problem. Looking for long-lost relative – that depends. But an experienced London detective who sets up an agency and then wants me to operate on the doubtful side of the law on his behalf? Come on! It smells – danger. I think the word is "entrapment".'

I leaned back as well, and shook my head. 'You are totally right, Sophia. But I'm the one who's trapped. I should never have taken this job. I don't speak the language. I don't know the people, and I'm out of my depth. I need your help. I'm offering you a large chunk of my fee because this should really have been your job in the first place.'

She said something to a waiter who was hovering, and he went away. She sat there looking at me, saying nothing for a long while, just as I looked at her. At last, she nodded, and said 'Money?'

I took an envelope out of my pocket and put it on the table. It vanished into her handbag, and she made a gesture with her hand. A young man got up from a distant table and came over.

'This is Andreas,'' she said. 'Give him your bag.' I nodded, and Andreas scooped my empty rucksack up and disappeared out of the café. The waiter came back with a glass of water and small cup filled with foaming brown sludge. 'What's this?' I asked as he put it down in front of me.

'Greek coffee. Medium sugar. The way you like your tea.'

That's when I realised I was dealing with a professional. She probably knew my inside leg measurement, and she probably wasn't impressed. I sipped the coffee. It wasn't filtered. It was like sucking bitter-sweet sand through my teeth.

'I have a few questions,' I said. 'Do you come from round here?'

She laughed. 'No, Johnny. I come from Athens.'

'Big city, I hear.'

'Athens was a city when London was a few mud-huts and a stinking river.'

'So, you're not local?'

'Did you think I was? The people here are peasants. Not long ago they had nothing but a few donkeys and some fishing boats. Now they have tourists and the internet. But they're still peasants. They are nothing like Athenians.'

'So why are you working on Corfu and not Athens?'

'I had an argument with my boss. This is a big agency. I got sent here. Crete would have been better.'

'You have nothing to do with the local families?'

She laughed, pulled a piece of paper out of her bag and handed it to me. Andreas came back in and put my rucksack down beside my chair. He was young, but strong, biceps straining his T-shirt. He went back to sit and watch from a distant table. Sophia, I realised, did not take chances. She looked to me like an ex-cop and she was prepared. For all I knew there was more back-up sitting around. And, of course, she was making a point. At my expense. Literally. Her English was perfect, with a slight

American tinge.

'As you can see,' she said, 'The *Artemis* is owned by the twin sisters Maria and Katerina, together with Katerina's ex-husband Spiros, and their uncle Vassilis Alexakis.'

'Anything known?' How easily I slipped back into the jargon.

'Yes,' she said. 'Uncle Vasillis owns a construction company and cement business. He has twice been fined for using a kind of concrete mix that's cheaper and not approved for building. Spiros is in prison.'

'What for?'

'Violent crime. He allegedly beat a man who took Vassilis to court over a holiday building that started to fall down soon after it was finished. There is some doubt about how true that is. That's all I know in the short time I've had.'

'I'm impressed. That's quick work.'

'We're a big company. Let's just say we have resources.'

I nodded. That was easy to decode. They had plenty of police contacts and probably access to the police database. Sophia was a tentacle of an organisation that could get pretty much whatever it wanted. I had a few mates, no passwords, no access, and bugger-all resources. If they wanted to play me, they could.

'Why did you leave the police?' I asked. Again, that pearly smile.

'Did I?'

'Listen, Sophia. I know I'm out of my depth here, but I'm not stupid. My nose tells me you were. You obviously know why I left. I'm interested in you. I need to know who I'm working with.'

'Shouldn't that be "whom"?'

'Yes, it bloody should. Who cares? Why did you leave?'

'May I give you a bit of advice, Johnny? Go back to London. Do what you're good at – and you were obviously good at it. You're about as much use here as a parrot at the south pole.'

She gave me another piece of paper.

'This is Andreas's mobile number. He'll be doing surveillance. I will be doing deep investigations. You will lie on the beach and await results. If you don't, from what I can see already, you'll be lying somewhere else trying to breathe concrete. All right?'

She'd been at least an Inspector, whatever that's called here. She was used to calling the shots, getting her own way, telling people what to do. She was definitely not a foot-soldier. If I made a move on her she would have kicked me in the crutch and had my damaged arm up behind my back before Andreas got within ten feet.

A breeze started the parasols flapping. She stood up, threw a euro note onto the table, and started walking away. As she passed me she put her hand gently on my shoulder and squeezed.

'I would have done what you did,' she said quietly. 'We'll be in touch.'

CHAPTER EIGHT

I took two small devices out of the bag Andreas has put into my rucksack, put the rest into a waterproof plastic Ziplock bag and made sure that it was safely snuggled at the bottom of the lavatory cistern. The owners were certain to have a master code for the little safe in the cupboard in the main room, where I'd put my passport and money. The gizmos were more or less transparent, and without sticking your hand into the cistern and groping you couldn't tell they were there. Nice one, Sophia. I texted her and ten minutes later she confirmed that the BMW parked across the road from *Artemis* belonged to Tina.

In the village, I went into the mini-market next to the bakery and bought another carton of milk, a big bottle of amazingly cheap red wine, oregano crisps, yoghurt, honey, and some water. Before I left I untied the bow on my left shoelace.

As I passed the BMW I pretended to notice it, swore, bent down, tied my shoelace, and slapped a tracker into the wheel-arch. That's not the greatest for signal, but it gets covered in crud very fast, and you'd need a power-jet and good eyes to spot it. Sleuthing is very high-tech these days, and I was used to that. Officially it was down to the nerds in the Met to handle this stuff, but I'd got on well with them on the whole and treated them like human beings, unlike some of my colleagues, who thought they were an alien species – which, to be fair, some of them were. Never accept an invite to play video games with a bunch of techies unless you want a lesson in abject humiliation. If they were half as good with a real gun as they were on-screen they should have been in Armed Response.

One down, one to go – for now.

She was behind the bar making cocktails for a bunch of Brits sitting at a table by the pool. She waved, and I waved back. I gestured something like opening a bottle and drinking, and she nodded. I dumped the shopping in my room and went back down. The pool-siders were happily poking themselves in the eye with little umbrellas and Maraschino cherries. I envied them – all they had to care about was where they were going to eat that night. I sat at the bar.

'How was Sidari?' she asked. The thing is, I sure as fuck hadn't told her I was going to Sidari. Was I blown already? 'I saw you get on the bus.'

I pulled a face. 'Not a patch on this place,' I said. 'More Butlins than Greece.'

'Good. I'm pleased you think so.'

'What's the Greek for *Where's the powder room*?'

'Oh. Get you! I thought only girls used the powder room.'

'I knew I was doing something wrong.'

'It's *poo ee-nay ee toileta*. You can just say it in English. The locals may not understand powder room, so try Where is it? Through the door and turn left.'

'Cheers.'

Did I tell you she was drop-dead gorgeous? She was Premier League. I was Scunthorpe United. She was polished and well-spoken. I was rough and chipped. But I still had this vision of getting into her knickers. Utterly stupid and totally unprofessional, but there was only one job one part of me had signed up for and he hadn't had a slimming job in the sea that day. *Don't*, I told myself. But I did.

'You're a very attractive woman, Tina.'

'Thank you. Now, excuse me.' The pool-siders were making gestures indicating imminent death by thirst. She gave them a thumbs-up and starting reaching for bottles and ice.

I waited until she had the drinks on a tray and headed inside. The office was right behind the bar and the door was open. I moved fast – in the main door, then left and into the office. I slapped a gizmo onto the top of the door frame, but it wouldn't stick. I had to press it down hard. Everything took twice as long with my left hand. Just as I got it settled she walked in.

'Why are you in here?'

'You said it was left. It must be second left. I nearly pissed in your filing cabinet.'

'Please don't.' No smile. Cool. Suspicious. Probably the real Tina. Best to play the idiot.

'This your office? Hell of a lot tidier than my desk ever was!' Big stupid grin. She relaxed slightly and nodded. I jiggled uncomfortably.

'Gotta go.'

'There's a big sign saying "W.C." over the door. Try not to miss! Oh, but you're a man so you will.'

I nodded, went out, went into the loos, and read the sign telling me not to put paper down the lav about six times while I had a slash. Then I went back outside, took my beer down beside the pool and stretched out on a sunbed. A blow-up giraffe was floating here and there as the breeze caught it.

'Better?' she asked as I put my bottle and glass back on the bar. She'd reverted to Ms Pleasant, but I knew that meant nothing.

Back upstairs I fired up the laptop. I'd already loaded it with software from the memory stick Sophia had provided, and I'd dropped the stick in the bottom of a waste bin in the ladies' loo downstairs. I entered two passwords from memory. After a few seconds the laptop connected to the bug in the office and I could hear the distant sounds of laughter from the pool area. I adjusted the slider down so that the mic wouldn't transmit until the sound was loud enough. Stage one completed.

I ran a second program. Google maps showed me the area around the *Artemis*, with a nice red blob sitting on the road outside: Tina's car.

The third program was obviously a bit more complicated, because it took a long time to do anything much except tell me to wait and showed a spinning disk. Meaningless techie words scrolled down in a box. Then it made a ping, and a green sign lit up. The software had control of the office router over the WiFi system. We could now access Tina's computer.

I clicked a button labelled "Redirect" and waited for a response. After about thirty seconds there was another ping and a green "connected" sign.

The burner phone rang. When I answered it Sophia said 'Don't touch anything. I'm getting the emails and other stuff. Andreas can track the car on his phone now. Eat at *Nafsika* at nine o'clock.'

'Where's that?'

'Just ask in the village. Bye.'

She hung up without waiting for me to reply. I took a shower and sat on the balcony drinking some wine and munching oregano crisps as the sun settled lower to the west. The breeze was stiffening, and looking down at the pool I could see the giraffe rammed up against the edge and the water looking disturbed. The sun-brollies were flapping. The sun-downers had gone. Tina came out and put them down, one by one, the skirt of her cotton dress blown tight around her perfectly-formed buttocks. Who are you, Tina? What are you? You are simultaneously of here and somewhere else. You are definitely not a *peasant*. Why are you serving drinks to tourists and not hosting dinner-parties in Kensington?

She went back into the bar and came out again with a bucket of white powder, which she threw into the pool. I watched it dissolve slowly in the rippling water. Then she headed back and was out of sight.

The sun was almost down as I reached the corner near the beach road and turned left into new territory, following the sign to the Port. A hundred yards later, past a couple of small bungalows, and there it was. The road ahead was flat and then rose up to a distant church. On my right was a restaurant called *Beachcomber* advertising mussels, and on the left, up an incline, was the *Nafsika Hotel.* It was a light cream rectangular building with two layers of balconies and a big restaurant at ground level. Outside, there were two low open buildings – just roofs with supporting wood pillars – which had chairs in a light blue shabby-chic style and tables with matching table-cloths. I went past the first building, where people were finishing their supper, and walked into the second. Two men were winding down thick transparent plastic sheets using an electric drill to form a wall against the breeze, which was heading towards being a wind. The setting sun splashed yellow on the plastic. Another man was clearing tables. I chose one in the corner where I could see everybody. At the far end there was a bar area. The paintings on the bar pillars were an odd mixture of brash, cartoonish girls pouting and delicate pastel images of what I assumed were classical figures and vases.

I'd ordered some wine and water and was looking at the menu when a strong-looking man in his fifties arrived beside me carrying a blackboard with inscriptions in various colours of chalk and held it up.

'Tonight's specials,' he said. Fair enough. Then he read them all out. Maybe they got a lot of blind people here, but, what the hell, it saved me the effort. 'We have the tzatziki - that's yoghurt and garlic, the kalamari – that's squid rings – the village sausage – and the mains we have the sea bass, the moussaka, the swordfish, the pastitsio – that's a local dish of pasta – and the grilled chicken with lemon potatoes.'

There was more, but I settled for the chicken, assured him that I'd ordered drinks, sat back, lit a cigarette. A young waiter arrived with a jug of plonk, poured some into my glass, cracked the bottle of water open and poured some into another glass, took a small plant out of the ashtray and put it near me, and put a basket of toast and a little bowl of something reddish on the table. I spread some on the toast. It was smoky crushed olives with some seasoning, and I pigged it.

People were sitting eating, mostly in couples, and there was a quiet buzz of chat. Wind was now rattling the plastic sheets

The chicken was moist with dark sear marks from the grill. Lemon potatoes? Bring it on. The lemony sauce from the potatoes worked perfectly with the chicken. I wasn't sure why I was here now, but I was definitely coming back. My hand was feeling good, and I found I could use it to drink the wine, although I had to use my other hand to pour it.

Sophia came in with a tall man wearing a light

suit and sat at the next table. She was wearing a dark blue dress with a silver brooch. Her hair was pinned up and she had light pink lipstick on. 'You don't know me. Stay there,' she said as she walked past.

They waved the owner's blackboard away and conversed with him in rapid Greek. He nodded, wrote down their order, and went away, coming back soon after with a bottle of white wine, which he presented proudly. The man studied it and nodded. Oh dear – I was clearly outclassed.

I took my time eating some water melon as a lot of different plates arrived on their table – fish-bites, a big bowl of cucumber and tomato with cheese on top, a pile of crispy lamb chops, stuff I couldn't recognise. It was making me hungry all over again just looking at it. Sophia managed to gnaw on a chop as though it were a delicacy – holding it in her hand by the bone with long fingers, which she wiped before sipping the straw-coloured wine.

Eventually they finished. Sophia looked at me and winked. The man stood up, came across and said 'Excuse me. Do you have a light?'

I flicked my lighter for him. 'How was the food?' I asked.

'Good. Surprisingly good. Staying here?'

'No – just eating.' He nodded, and said 'I'm Yiannis and that is Sophia.' She smiled at me.

'Johnny. Johnny Almond.'

'On your own?' she asked, and I nodded. 'Why

don't you come and join us? For a drink.'

'I don't want to intrude,' I said without much conviction.

He pulled out a chair at their table and said something to the waiter, who was starting to clear their plates away. In the gaps between the low background music I could hear waves breaking on the shore. Through the plastic sheeting I could see a couple of people walking out of the arch of the place across the road, and could just make out *Taverna O Manthos* written around the arch. The waiter reappeared with a clean wine-glass for me, and Yiannis poured some of their bottle into it.

'Try this,' he said. It had a hint of flowers in its scent. It smelt expensive. It tasted delicious – dry and kind of flinty.

'That,' I said 'is wonderful.'

'Isn't it? It's an Assyrtiko wine from Santorini.'

Those of us who've spent our lives condemned to apparent ignorance because we have working-class roots can spot when we're being patronised from across the horizon.

'Of course,' I said, "When Thera blew up in a massive eruption and destroyed the Minoan civil-isation it left behind fertile volcanic soil for later generations, so maybe the acidity is a hint of the pain of King Minos. Perhaps, even, his guilt.'

I'd decided – if that's the right word – to dis-like Yiannis. Probably just childish jealousy – I'm good at that. And anyway, all my alarm bells were still ringing. Why were they here, nearly an hour's drive from Corfu Town? I didn't think they'd come just to eat. And all my instincts told me they were not a couple.

Yiannis hijacked the owner on his way past – and Spiros (it turned out) came back with a different bottle. It was examined, studied, discussed, and then opened. Fresh glasses appeared.

Spiros turned to me. 'This, Sir, is from *Monemvasia* at the southern tip of the Peloponnese. Try it.'

I was getting the impression that I'd been summoned to a pissing-up-the-wall contest with the Greeks, which was only confirmed when Yiannis said 'People think Greek wine is a joke. But we've been creating wonderful wines for three thousand years.'

'Maybe you need to get better at selling them,' I said. 'The French have literally got you over a barrel.'

Sophia's mouth crinkled at the edges. She was enjoying this.

'We keep the best for ourselves. Food, wine, women.'

I smiled at Sophia. 'That's obvious,' I said.

CHAPTER NINE

The second bottle was very nice, but wasn't helping my peace of mind. When everybody else, including Spiros and the waiters, had repaired to the bar I leaned forward and said 'Okay. Let's cut to the chase. Why are you here?' I gestured to Yiannis. 'And who exactly are you?'

I didn't mention that I'd spotted the Glock in a shoulder holster under his left armpit. Little as I knew about Greece I assumed that private detectives weren't generally permitted to wander around with hand-guns.

He looked me in the eye and said 'Exactly what did Maria Alexaki say to you in London?'

'I believe I already told Sophia that. And I still don't know who you are.'

'We'll get to that. Her exact words?'

'She said her sister was in deep shit. She wanted me to make discreet inquiries so that she could help her sister.'

'That's it?'

'Pretty much. She said she wasn't sure what was going on. I was not to interfere, just report back. I must never reveal that I was working for her.'

Sophia chipped in. 'From what we can gather, the sisters hate each other. So why would Maria be concerned?'

'I don't know. Yet. You tell me.'

'Two girls with lots of money behind them. They live in West London. They go to the Lady Eleanor Holles girls' private school in Hampton. One goes to university and medical school and becomes a doctor. The other leaves school with good examination grades, goes into the airline business and becomes cabin crew, then comes to Corfu and becomes a rep for a while. Then she gives that up and runs a property business with their uncle. Maybe not such a clean property business. They are happy twins, doing what they want to do.

'While Maria and her husband are visiting Corfu, Katerina sleeps with Maria's husband. Maria finds out. Maria is a highly respectable doctor, but she wants revenge. She seduces Katerina's husband. Both the girls get divorced.

'It's a scandal in the village. The Alexakis family do not like scandal. Apart from a bit of vagueness over the tax laws they are a well-off, efficient group of people who stick together.'

Yiannis poured some more wine. 'What Sophia means is the family is split. But they will help the ones they don't like if they have to.'

'I know what you are,' I said. 'You're not a private detective.'

He put his hands up, pleading innocence. 'I am a VERY private detective!'

I leaned back and looked at them both. 'You, Yiannis, are either serious crime squad, or whatever you call it here, or you're an intelligence officer. Probably Sophia as well.'

'Did you ever really leave the police?' Sophia said. 'In your head? I don't think so. We don't think so.'

She tossed the envelope of money I'd given her onto the table. 'You have a choice, Johnny. Either tell Maria you can't do it and go back to London. Or work with us. We'll double your fee. We need you.'

'You don't trust Maria?'

'We don't trust anybody. Not even you.'

The wine was turning to acid in my stomach. Tina might be in deep shit, but I was at the sewage farm and barely swimming.

'Do I get a Glock G45?'

They laughed. I knew they would.

As I walked back the wind was howling and the sea sounded angry. A big black Mercedes with darkened windows passed me at high speed and vanished round the bend. There were no stars and the street lights were wobbling. Somewhere, shutters banged and a couple of dogs skulked home with their ears down.

I paused where the harbour road met the beach road opposite a mini-market and turned down towards the sea. I needed to think, and think hard. The car park was empty. The sea was roaring in with lashing foam over the sand. And out over the islands there were sudden strokes of violet lightning. If ever I had felt alone, I felt alone there.

There are always those moments in CID when you realise that every little sandcastle of theory you'd built up about a case was crumbling. But there, in the office or in the pub, you could kick it around with the others and maybe come up with another approach.

Standing on that shore that night I had no team I could trust. I was as good as a beachball in the gale. So, I had a choice: give up, put my tail between my legs, and go home – or stay and see which way it went. If I gave up I would have to give Maria back the money she'd spent, and to be honest, I needed it. I hadn't been in business long. Fair enough, I'd had a decent pay-out from the Met and a generous pension, but I wasn't about to retire before I was fifty, thank you very much. Of course, I could write a scandalous book about sloppy practice and shagging in the Force, and I toyed with that idea. That was for later.

The thing is – I am a persistent sod. To be a detective, you need to be, because the truth is usually buried under a large trawler-full of red herrings, and you need to strip the scales off one by one. You need to be stubborn, and your evidence needs to be good enough for the CPS and the court. You don't know whether there's a needle in the hay-stack until you've sifted through the whole tedious pile. And every step has to be written-up and obviously sensible because if you made a glorious cluster-fuck of it the internal investigation team would take you apart and nail your bollocks to the station front wall.

Sometimes you feel like everything's against you – the criminals, your friends, your colleagues, your management. You make a choice – go with the party line or follow the instinct that told you there was *something* to be found.

The sea was racing in, flooding the little lakes by the empty parking area on the beach. The wind was bending the bamboos along the fringe almost horizontal. I could feel salt spray in my face. The lightning strikes out to sea were lighting the clouds with blue and white.

I made my decision. I would do what I came here to do, and I turned and headed into the village, the wind behind me, urging me on.

In England, rain announces itself quietly at first – some drizzle, a few drops, a sudden chill. Things didn't work like that here. Do you remember the Ice Bucket Challenge that swept England a few years ago? You sat like a complete prat while somebody behind you tipped a bucket of freezing water over you. You survived. You got a round of applause like you'd won the Battle of Britain single-handed and knocked out Mohammed Ali in round one.

As I was walking passed *Peli and Maria*'s paper shop it went from not raining to a little like drowning within a second. Heavy drops were bouncing off the road like shattered glass, and by the time I'd covered the short distance past the now-dark *Little Prince* and *El Greco* and reached *Tasty Corner* the main street was a river pouring down into a whirlpool. My trainers were soaked. I was soaked. There was no point in taking shelter, and I sploshed on up to my ankles in water. There was a huge flash and a deafening bang. I wondered if I was dead. Then I wondered why not. The rain was so heavy I couldn't see through it – it was battering me. Lightning's electricity, right? Water conducts electricity. I was now half-way up to my knees in water and Christ knows how many billion volts were out to get me.

The light from the street-lamps was fighting a losing battle as I fought my way upstream towards *Artemis*. Water was pouring down the steps up from the road, and the swimming pool was a thousand little fountains in the light from below.

In my room I stripped off, dumped my wet clothes into the shower-room, wrapped a towel around myself. I was shivering. Armageddon was raging outside. But the balcony was sheltered and dry. There was no way I was going to sleep through this, and anyway, the night's events had left me tense and edgy. I rescued my cigarettes and lighter from my wet clothes. Some of the cigarettes had turned into a brown mush, but a few were smokable. I dried the lighter on some bog paper, lit up, and sat outside watching the fireworks with a glass of wine, despite the obvious fact that I'd had plenty.

The flashes were coming about every thirty seconds, but steadily they became less violent and the gap between the flash and the thunder grew longer. It was passing up the valley on its way to who knows where? The rain eased off and the wind dropped. I went inside, read my book for a bit, and dropped off to an unsettled sleep.

CHAPTER TEN

I'd left the curtains open when I went to bed, probably out of some primitive instinct that if you could see lightning it wasn't hitting you. It was bright outside when I woke up, but cooler, and the violent wind had dropped to nothing. Below me the pool was flat calm, and sunbeds were drying in the morning sun. I made some toast and sat on the balcony with a cup of tea, then went inside and brought the laptop back to life.

I scanned the tracker data. Tina had left *Artemis* at six-thirty, stopped at a supermarket, and then gone up to near Avliotes and into a village nearby, where she'd stayed for the night. That was probably where she lived, or at least somewhere she shared a bed. I'd have to check that out. In other words, routine surveillance stuff – but not so easy for me with no car. Maybe Andreas had already checked it out. I sent him a text, and he replied 'No.' But Andreas was working for Sophia, and I had to be wary of him.

There was a knock on the door, then a turning key and it opened. It was the maid, carrying a mop and big plastic rubbish sack.

'Sorry,' she said, backing out. I beckoned her back in and smiled. 'It's okay.' She nodded, went into the bathroom, emptied the loo-paper bin into her sack, mopped the floor, dumped the bag outside on the corridor, came back in and made my bed with startling speed and efficiency. I could never get sheets flat at the best of times, but you try it with one hand!

I pointed to the bed and gave my biggest grin. 'Fantastic, I said, and smiled. She made an "it's nothing" gesture and left, closing the door behind her.

One of the phones rang, and when I answered it Maria said 'Any news?'

'Nothing yet, I'm afraid.'

'I'm relying on you, Johnny. Don't spend too long lying on the beach. How's the hand?'

'Strange to tell, it's a lot better, thank you.'

'Good. I thought it would be. The sunlight promotes vitamin D production, and that's excellent for nerve growth and the immune system. Eat plenty of tomatoes and try not to live off gyros and pizza.'

'Yes, doctor.'

'Take an hour off and walk up to Akrotiri. It's a great view. I recommend the smoked salmon salad.'

'How do I get there.'

'Ask Tina. I'll call you tomorrow.'

She rang off.

Tina was re-stocking the fridge in the bar. She was wearing a loose saffron-coloured dress and had silver bangles on her wrists. She ticked all the boxes, but I didn't feel the slightest flicker of desire, just a cold mathematical assessment of how dangerous she was. The hard ice of yesterday had given way to a broad charming smile.

'How are you today, Johnny?'

'I thought I was going to die last night in that storm.'

'They come, sometimes, but they don't usually last long. Much worse is the wind we call the *maistro*. That blows for three days and you can hardly stand up. Now look – another lovely day in paradise. The sea will be a bit cooler until tomorrow. Where did you go to eat last night?'

'I think it's called *Nafsika*.'

'Bet you don't know who Nafsika was.'

'I have no idea.'

'According to Homer, on his way back from *Troy* Odysseus was shipwrecked on the island of *Scheria*, which we like to believe was Corfu. He was rescued by the king's daughter – Nafsika. They fell in love and he stayed for seven years, then ditched her and went home to his wife.'

'What an arsehole.'

'They all were. Don't mention it around here, but the Greek heroes were a bunch of piratical thieving murdering untrustworthy brutes. How was the food?'

'Good?'

'Very good.'

She leaned her elbows on the bar. 'Spiros went to college in New York. His father made his money selling hamburgers there. How did you get on with him?'

That was an odd question, and I wasn't sure how to answer. 'Fine,' I said. 'He knows a lot about wine.'

'He knows a lot about a lot of things. Now and then he gets a bit impatient. So do I.'

'Me too.'

She laughed. 'And me. You'd be amazed how stupid some people can be. Only this morning somebody wanted a refund because they couldn't sleep last night with the thunder. Apparently, we should have said that on our website.'

'I must admit I was soaked to the skin. My trainers are still damp. But I reckoned it was a pretty good free light-show.'

'Corfu gets more rain than Manchester, but we don't advertise that. Most of it's in the winter, anyway.'

'Fair enough. Oh – there was something I wanted to ask you. Some people last night said I should go to *Akrotiri*. How do I get there? Do I need a taxi?'

'*Akrotiri*'s a bar up on the headland. Walk a bit into the village. When you pass *Vaso and Yianni*'s restaurant there's a track going up the hill. When you reach the top, turn right. It's beautiful up there. It's a bit steep, but worth it.'

*

God, was I out of shape. The path was a rutted sandy track. As I climbed there was a hedge on my right with blackberry bushes and to the left was a field with long grass and flowers of every colour.

I was getting short of breath and my calves were complaining. The steepest thing in Stokey was the slope down to the pond in Clissold Park, and that was a snooker table compared to this.

As I stopped to get my wind, she came past me: late-thirties, blonde pony-tail, long legs, orange T-shirt and red shorts, turquoise trainers and ankle-socks. It couldn't be, could it?

She slowed down, turned her blue eyes towards me, and said 'Beat you to the top, Johnny!'

Detective Sergeant Suzanne "Goldilocks" Jones, my partner in unorthodox policing, unfulfilled sexual fantasy for every straight bloke in the Stokey nick, and probably most of the gay women. Looking at Suzanne you'd think she was a nice gentle girl from somewhere vaguely north of Watford who probably liked flower-arranging and aspired to be a vicar's wife. She'd got a First in Modern Languages from Leeds University, and if she kicked a perp in the balls they stayed down screaming for a long time. She enjoyed that. Some prick in Uniform tried it on in the canteen once, and he was off work for a week.

'What the fuck are you doing here, Suzi?' I shouted, as she sprinted away. I engaged first gear and ran after her. Call me an unreconstructed male chauvinist if you want, but I hate being beaten by a woman. I pounded up the hill, only just behind her, lungs heaving, legs heading for a painful meltdown. Her pony-tail bobbed up and down.

Then she stopped and pointed to the left. There

was a hollow, and a low building surrounded by swings, big wooden artificial flowers, strange sculptures, brightly-painted chairs.

'Buddhist creative retreat, that is. Just what you need. Know the old Zen saying "What is the sound of a one-handed clap?" That would suit you. You've gone flabby. Bit of chanting and bead-rattling should be right up your street.'

At the top of the track we came to a rough road that ran along the top of the headland. We walked up a stony rise and suddenly there was a low building with what looked like sails over a wide terrace. The garden was full of huge pots and flowers amidst benches and tables with cushions. The views were spectacular – *Agios Stefanos* on one side and the village of *Arillas* on the other. Out in the vast sea the islands gleamed in the sunlight.

Fit-looking Germans wearing shorts and stout shoes were eating lunch and conversing.

'This is beautiful,' I said.

'Isn't it just. Great sunsets up here.'

A tall, strong-looking man with a bald head welcomed us with a big smile and showed us to a table in the shade of the terrace under the sails. Suzi ordered two smoked-salmon salads and a bottle of *retsina* and we sat and ate, talked about the old days and shared a few laughs at the expense of our erstwhile colleagues. The distant sea was the same blue as her eyes.

Then she said 'Do you want to carry on being a small-time PI or do you want to get back into action, Johnny? I really don't see you lasting long before you go totally gaga.'

'Meaning what?'

'There's far more to all this than you know at present. Would you like to be useful?'

'I have no desire to go back into the police.'

'That's not it. Not by a long chalk.'

CHAPTER ELEVEN

Word of advice. If Suzanne Jones offers you a lift on a quad-bike, just say no. Maybe you think you're tough and you like hanging upside down on a fairground ride. Maybe you've flown F-111 fighters in a combat zone without so much as a tremble. Fought off three hundred Taliban with nothing more than a cocktail stick?

I promise you, you will shit yourself.

She'd had it parked next to the bar. 'How come?' I asked. 'You didn't know I was coming up here.'

'There's another one on the beach. And a car opposite *Little Prince*.'

She drove flat-out along the headland, over ruts and pot-holes, the engine roaring and stone spitting out behind the quad. I had my arms wrapped tight around her stomach and her pony-tail blowing in my face. There were five-hundred-foot cliffs to the left and a steep drop into the valley on the right. She didn't give a shit about physics. Or death.

The thing about Suzi is she's not arrogant. She just does things. She does them very well. I'd never found anything she couldn't do but presumably she just didn't do them. She pulled up near the big house at the end of the promontory in a hail of sand and stones and slipped neatly off the bike. When I stood up my legs were shaky and the vibrations of the engine seemed to carry on in my buttocks.

She walked over to the cliff edge and stood looking out to sea. 'Decided yet?'

'How did you know I was here?'

'I asked for you. To help me. I phoned *The Prince* and asked Dominic if he'd seen you. He said last he heard you were off to Corfu on holiday. After that it was easy. Your ticket was booked on-line, you confirmed your passenger details with the airline, including where you were staying. Bit of hacking. Piece of piss, really.'

'What's going on, Suzi?'

'No join, no tell. That's the way it works.'

'I have conditions.' She turned and looked at me. 'What conditions?'

'You will drive at no more than twenty miles an hour if I'm on the back. You will stop being a smug know-it-all. You will tell me the fucking truth.'

She turned and kissed me on the cheek. 'Deal. Bit boring, but needs must.' She pulled a mobile out of her bum-bag, speed-dialled a number, and handed it to me.

It was answered immediately, and a suave male voice said 'You agree, Inspector Almond?'

'Didn't seem like I had a choice.'

'It's always a choice. Have you made it?'

'Catch-22 isn't it? If I'm going to make a choice I need to know what's happening. But unless I say Yes you won't tell me.'

'Very good assessment. We were going to approach you earlier, but your unfortunate – erm –

accident caused a bit of a wobble.'

'Who's We exactly?'

'In general, I'd say it was UK Intelligence. Under the circumstances I'd say that we can extend that to the world.'

'Which tells me fuck-all.'

'Of course.'

'Who's in charge. Me or Suzi?'

'I am. You will have equal rank.'

'Who are you?'

Oh – let's see – you can think of me as the Fat Controller. Seriously, John, you have skills we need. I don't think Suzi would have pleaded with me to bring you in if you hadn't.'

She'd been listening to all this, her lips firmly pressed together. 'Okay, Fat Controller, 'I said.

'Excellent.'

The phone went dead. I handed it to Suzi. 'Pleaded?'

'Get over it, Johnny. Really.'

She drove the quad very slowly a couple of hundred yards back down the track and stopped. She slipped off, and said 'That sedate enough for you?'

'Piss off.'

She beckoned, and we walked through the scrubby trees up a little incline. We came to a small white church – well – to be accurate, a tiny church. The door was open. Inside, there were icons hanging on the wall: Jesus, the Virgin, and sundry figures whom I assume were saints. There was a sandbox with some dead candles in it, and nearby a box of slender new candles and some matches. She took a candle from the box, lit it, and fixed it upright in the sand.

'I didn't know you were religious.'

'I'm not. I just reckon we need all the help we can get.'

I pointed to the array of saints. 'They're not impressed,' I said. She sighed that way women have when you are being uncooperative and walked out, with me trailing behind.

There were loads of pebbles around the church with writing on them. She sat down against the church wall and handed me a pebble as I joined her. The sun was past overhead but bright and hot on our faces. She pointed to the writing on the pebble.

'This says "Angelos we pray for you." When somebody dies you might come up here, light a candle, and leave a prayer on a pebble. I like it.'

I smiled. 'So do I. What I would prefer is a pebble written in English telling me what's going on.'

'Fair enough. There are hints and fragments and little cryptic pebbles that indicate that something awful is being planned by mostly unknown people for unknown reasons. But it involves the UK as well as Greece. One hint suggests that this region is important.

'Brexit cut the UK off from Interpol and policing. But Intelligence never went along with this. Too many connections. Too much at stake.

'You are not here by accident, Johnny. You have perfect cover. You are plainly handicapped. You are an ex-cop and a struggling private eye who could do with a bit of time in the sun to get his raw pastry complexion up to something approximately human.

'You have a unique ability to put two and two together and work out what three is. I've seen you do it. Many times. I don't know how you do it, and I don't think you do. You kind of smell it. Like a male dog can smell a bitch in heat from miles away.'

'Pick another analogy, Suzi. I'm not sure I like that one.'

'We were the best team, Johnny. We were the A Team. We pissed-off our colleagues because we were too bloody good at it. For this we have to be A Star. We have to find out what's going on, where, how and when. Look – I'll admit I'm clever. I can do logic. I can do languages. But I don't have your *feel*. The hidden part of your brain works better than mine – better than most.'

I sat back against the warm wall listening to the cicadas chirp in the foliage. Her hair was gleaming in the sunlight. After a bit I said 'I expect you have a plan.'

'Suggestion. Not plan.'

'Go on.'

'We meet in the village. We have a romance. That means we can be seen together. This is a small place. People watch people. They'll be more interested in whether we slept together than anything else. They'll be taking bets on how long it will last. We will be known, but *not* known. In public, you'll be besotted with me. In private you'll probably be an arsehole.'

'If I'm going to be besotted I'll need acting classes.'

'I'm sure you can manage *arsehole* without assistance.'

We sat there for half an hour or more arguing about the way to do it. Having lunch in *Akrotiri* was not really a problem because everybody else there appeared to be German, and we knew from experience that after a few days people's memory of times and dates gets confused and inaccurate.

My proposal did not go down well. The Arsenal were playing Spurs in the North London derby at seven-thirty Greek time, and I'll already checked that it was on the satellite channel at *El Greco*'s and the *Princess Bar*. Perfect place for an accidental meeting, I thought. Suzi scoffed at the idea. Suzi, as I knew from long nights sitting in an unmarked car with her, judged a football team on how good looking its best-looking player was. I pointed out that The Arsenal was composed of god-like beings and I was surprised the Greeks hadn't got around to putting up statues of them.

'The trouble with you, Suzi, is you have lousy taste.'

She sighed. 'Oh, so true, Johnny boy. How long does it last?'

'Ninety minutes, for Christ's sake. I thought you knew everything.'

'Only everything that matters. Ninety minutes

is too long. Does that include their beer break half-way through?'

'No.'

'Overpaid load of wankers, if you ask me.'

On a bad day at the Emirates about fifty thousand people would have agreed with her, but I sure as fuck wasn't going to tell her that. Every plan she came up with was crap, and she knew it. We made a deal. Under no circumstances whatsoever was I going to wear the Arsenal Away shirt I'd brought with me. She was not required to shout, wave things, or in any way express more than mild interest, however sublime the passing was. We should be noticed, of course, but I was not to emit loud expletives or behave like a demented yob. I was to behave, however unlikely it seemed, like a *quite* attractive well brought-up man with whom no decent and intelligent woman would spurn the opportunity of dinner.

Tough call. How can you watch the Gooners and not feel the blood run through like hot lava?

She imposed even more conditions.

'Wear trousers. Definitely not shorts.'

'Why?'

'Just do it.'

'Why?'

'Do I have to spell it out?'

'That's what "why" means.'

'I am, for the purposes of this task, Suzanne Jones – an educated ex-journalist who is renting a little house here to write a novel. There is no way this Suzanne Jones would be seen dead after dark with a man who was wearing shorts – let alone one with hairy knees who looked like you.'

'You are such a bitch.'

'Yep.'

I was in place at seven fifteen at a table near the screen in *The Princess Bar*. It's a part of the *Little Prince* taverna and apartments, but separated from it by the main path up to the entrance. It was big inside, and had lots of tables and chairs with brollies outside. There were couples sipping variously-coloured pre-dinner drinks. I had a Mythos and a little bowl of crisps nearby. On the TV the camera panned across ranks of Spurs supporters and I had a strong impulse to scream at them. It's like that. You know it's just a game but you know it isn't. It's tribal. To me, the Emirates is a cathedral, and these infidels in their dreary white shirts and bobble-hats were an offence to the sacred ground.

We were ten minutes in when she turned up. I'd actually forgotten about her. Our defence had gone AWOL as usual and Spurs were getting cross after cross in. Then we broke – poetry in motion – sweeping forward, a long ball to the right, some jinking, a high fast cross, and Saka put a header into the net that was so beautiful they should have hung it in the Louvre.

I jumped up and shouted 'YES!!!!!' One nil to The Arsenal. Joy unbounded.

A woman's voice shouted 'Brilliant!' and I turned around to see who it was. She was wearing a red top of some crinkly material and a long amber silk skirt. She had big white bangles in her ears and lipstick. I had never seen Suzi wearing lipstick. Never.

She came to the table and said for all to hear 'You mind if I join you? Seem to be a lot of the enemy about.'

Within seconds a gin and tonic arrived on the table beside her and some more crisps. She smiled up at the man with nice crinkly eyes who'd brought it and said '*Echfareestoe Michal*i' or words to that effect. He said something that sounded like parrots in the loo, and went away. Not, I noticed, before giving her shoulder a little stroke.

As planned we didn't talk until half-time. Michalis brought more drinks and gave her shoulder an even bigger stroke.

'It's not very exciting, is it?' she said. 'I think we'd be better off playing four-three-three. They're getting down the channels far too easily. We're not playing through the mid-field. The strikers are having to drop back too deep and they can't get any space in front.'

'You've been reading Mark Lawrenson.'

'Yes. Research.'

'I'm sorry. I don't know your name.'

'Suzi.'

'Hi Suzi. I'm Johnny.'

We shook hands. I used my right hand, and she took it very gently. It went downhill from there. Spurs rampaged down the pitch smacking the ball from one side to the other. Our defence had obviously been taking sleeping pills at half time and we were subjected to close-ups of the net shaking. By the time the final whistle blew we were down three-two. Suzi was smirking next to me.

'Try to look upset.'

'I am.'

'Try harder.'

'Do you actually pay to go and watch this? I knew you were a tosser but I didn't know you were a masochist.'

'Let's go and eat.'

'Now that is a good idea. I suggest we eat here. Good place to be spotted.'

We moved across to the other half of the building and got the same table that I'd had before on the platform. Andy and Gill were at their table next to a pillar for a front-row seat of the dancing. Gill smiled at me in a knowing sort of way and nodded her approval.

Suzi had eaten an entire meal by the time I was on my third bit of chicken kebab. I have never had any idea how she did it. She wasn't fat, she wasn't big. Every man within range had run his eyes over her. She looked – well – demure. She did not look like five foot six of violent retribution waiting for an excuse to rabbit punch somebody.

It was midnight when I walked her along past the dark and silent paper-shop. We said goodbye at a respectful distance and she walked away up the slope into the night.

I retraced my steps past the paper shop, the coffee bar, which was still busy, past *Little Prince*. I was level with *Tasty Corner* when I heard shouting from up the main street.

The *Silver Moon* bar is on the corner, then up the road is the bakery, then a supermarket and then the stream. It runs between the *Barras* on the right and the *Thomas Bay Hotel*, under the road, and down to the sea through a stand of bamboos. It's about ten feet below street level, with vertical concrete sides and no way down. That's where a crowd was gathering. People were running across the road and out of some bars.

As a detective you respond to things like this in two ways: part of you says "You'd better investigate," and the other part says "Sod it. Leave it to Uniform." There didn't seem to be any uniform in evidence, so I turned up the road and joined the steady line of people heading for the stream. A woman with high heels and a mini-skirt was being violently sick in the road. A waiter was carrying a ladder over from the *Thomas Bay*.

I managed to get near enough to the fence to see what the yelling was about. Below the railings a shadowy form was lying face down on the concrete bottom of the stream. The sound of a siren grew rapidly in the distance and then a police car came down the hill at about sixty with its blues flashing and screeched to a halt in the middle of the road. Two cops jumped out and started shouting at people to keep away. One of them leaned over the railings and shouted to the other one, who opened the boot and came back seconds later with a large torch.

The first cop grabbed the ladder from the waiter and climbed over the fence next to the supermarket. He lowered the ladder into place against the side-wall of the stream and climbed down into the gloom, his partner following him.

It was a powerful torch. The light played over the body. Definitely male physique. Blood gleamed in the trickle of water and detergent bubbles flowing past him. Lots of blood. The policemen debated for a minute and then turned him over. Probably against regulations, but I didn't blame them.

The torch beam played over the gash across his throat. There were screams and gasps from the crowd around me. Cold fingers of something primitive ran up my spine.

Andreas.

CHAPTER TWELVE

Tina's car was parked outside the *Artemis* when I got back. That was odd. She wasn't usually there this late. But the office was dark and locked when I went inside. I backtracked out of the door and walked far enough back to get a view of the building. There was only one light on – the far-left room on the top floor. I could just see the gleam through the shutters. The light went out.

I moved across the pool area and slid silently behind some bushes next to a barbecue, crouching in the shadows. Thirty seconds later she came out of the building, walking fast. She looked tense and strained in the blue light from under the pool. There was a handbag on her shoulder – nothing else.

A minute passed and I heard the car start up and drive away.

Back in my room I phoned Sophia's number. She answered immediately. 'I'm just eating. Is it important?'

I'd already discovered that the Greeks were nocturnal and thought one in the morning was a good time to have a nosh. Over supper, clever clogs Suzi had made a joke about owls being the symbol of the goddess Athena.

'Sorry to say this. Andreas is dead. He's in the stream in the village with his throat cut.'

There was a deafening banging. She'd dropped her mobile. I waited. When she picked it up again I knew she was crying and she shouted in Greek to somebody else. Through her tears she said 'You must be very careful. I'll call you in the morning, John. Sorry. It's a shock. Andreas is my nephew.'

After I'd put the phone down I checked the tracker on Tina's car. She'd gone home at six as usual, but then she went out again. She'd gone through *Avliotes* and towards the coast on the west, where she'd stopped for over an hour. At that point the tracker went dead, and the screen just showed "Trace lost. Device ceased transmission."

I poured a glass of wine, then thought better of it, poured it down the handbasin in the bathroom and made a cup of tea. The balcony doors were open. I closed them and locked them, then jammed a dining chair under the door handle. I didn't think Andreas would have put my details on his mobile, but it was always a risk. Should I call Suzi? I decided not to. As far as I knew there was no connection between Andreas and Suzi, and I needed her fresh and awake in the morning.

Can't say I really slept. I shuffled about uneasily on the bed, senses alert in some subliminal way, wearing a pair of shorts because facing an attacker bollock-naked doesn't feel good. I had no weapons; my right hand was a liability more than an asset and they don't teach you much left-handed unarmed combat at the Police Academy at Hendon. I wasn't prepared for violence. Everything I'd assumed when I came out here had turned out to be way off-beam.

At five o'clock one of the phones vibrated. Sophia had got her act together. 'Don't worry about Andreas's mobile,' she said. 'If anybody tries to hack it will burst into flames. But keep a low profile. Very low. Understand?'

'Of course. What you could do is check the hospitals for anybody with burns on their hands.'

'There's only one hospital at *Kontokali*, just north of Corfu town. We have two people there and we're watching their computers. I'll let you know. Go to the beach and be a tourist until we have more information. I'll call you.'

'Got it.'

She hung up. I paced around for a bit, made some more tea, had a shower, checked the door, and eventually opened the balcony doors and went outside. There was hazy cloud and a couple of jet contrails out towards the sea. Back inside I took the chair away from the door and went out into the corridor. I checked the room numbers. Either it was a coincidence, or Tina had been in room twelve last night.

I made another cup of tea, grabbed some biscuits, pulled a T-shirt on, and went downstairs. There were little white tables beside the sunbeds, with cup-shaped depressions for drinks. I settled my tea in one, put a phone beside it on the table, stretched out on the sunbed and started watching the apartment block. One by one the balcony doors opened and the guests came out and checked the towels hanging over the balcony rails or brought their breakfast out. Alan and his wife strolled down and claimed their usual beds on the other side of the pool with a cheerful wave.

Just before ten Tina came in and opened the bar. Her face was a little drawn, but she was still outstandingly beautiful. The shutters on room twelve remained closed. I knew that hotels sometimes kept a room free for storage or because the plumbing was bust, but I couldn't think of any reason why Tina would be in there late at night – she was usually out of the place at six as fast as a load of kids when the bell went at the end of the school day.

I'd already texted Suzi to meet me at the beach at eleven. She replied with just one word – *Mistral*. That rang a bell and I remembered that there was a sign saying "Mistral" across the road from *Nafsika*. I took my empty mug up to my room and packed my Speedos, flip-flops and a towel in my rucksack.

There was police no-entry tape around the culvert next to the supermarket as I walked down the road. In the paper shop I bought a carton of cigarettes from a friendly woman with fair hair who spoke excellent English. Turned out she was one of the two sisters who owned the place, and she was called Maria.

'Why so many Marias and so many Spirosses?' I asked her. She laughed.

'Spiros after the island saint – Saint Spyridon.

Maria because we are all virgins.'

Somehow, I doubted it.

'I'm Johnny,' I told her.

'Another saint, then! How long are you staying?'

'Until I'm no longer a virgin.'

'The winters can be quite cold. Don't waste any time.'

'Listen - What's all that police stuff in the village?'

'I think it was an accident. Somebody local. No need to worry, Johnny. Here – I will give you a lighter.'

That was obviously going to be the party line in the village. Bleeding bodies dumped in a ditch are not good for business. But she was right. This had bugger-all to do with the tourists, but nobody wanted to stay in a place where a man got his throat cut, even if it was local affair. Nobody went to Yorkshire on Jack the Ripper holidays, did they? Not that I'd ever been to Yorkshire.

I walked on down to the beach, turned left when I reached the stream, and through some parked cars. There was an array of sunbeds outside the *Waves* taverna. There were some plank walkways, and I crossed through, across a gap to a much smaller patch of sunbeds with shady straw brollies along the beach to the left. The beach was wide here – hard-packed sand – and then the sea, fringed with a beard of black seaweed.

The sunbeds were in pairs with a small plastic table underneath. They were semi-permanent affairs with a straw or reed canopy and a sturdy trunk, four rows of eight. The sand was brushed smooth around them. Suzi was stretched out on the last bed, wearing a light-blue bikini, reading a paperback in the shade. I walked very quietly between the beds towards her.

'You're crap, Johnny,' she said. 'I clocked you a mile away.'

'Glad you're keeping up with your skills,' I said. 'You're going to need them.'

I sat on the bed next to hers, spread my towel over my loins, and changed into my Speedos while I briefed her on last night's events. She thought for a bit, turned on her side towards me and said 'Why dump him there? Was it a warning?'

'Exactly my thought. The question is, who were they warning?'

'No reason to think it was us. But we should consider ourselves warned.'

I got up, adjusted the tilt on my sunbed, leaned down and kissed the top of her head.

'What was that for?'

'We're supposed to be starting a holiday romance. Didn't your mother tell you it usually involves a bit of a snog?'

'Oh. Like Beauty and the Beast, you mean?'

'Thanks. It's a while since anybody called me Beauty. Now – let's get to it. We'll have to manage without a white-board. And the first thing is, what is it you are not telling me?'

She looked me in the eye and said 'You know as

much as I do, Johnny. All I've been told is that there is something going down that seems to be centred in this area. Whatever it is it can't just be a police matter or the security services wouldn't be interested, would they? They need eyes on the ground here, and any Greek would stick out like a sore thumb. Our brief is to survey and stay out of it.'

I stretched out on the bed and put my hands behind my head.

'And if the shit hits the fan? Like it did for Andreas?'

'We improvise. If necessary we get the fuck out of here and call it in.'

''Where to?'

'London. We can't really trust anybody else.'

'Can we trust London?'

'Who pays the piper?'

'Okay. I need a swim. Come on.'

She looked worried. 'You go. I'll stay here.'

'We need to talk. Let's go.'

'Johnny, you are not my superior anymore.'

'Thanks for reminding me. There's somebody on the path to the left, where there's a little road going up towards the church. He's got binoculars. I saw the flash on the lenses. Maybe he can lip-read.'

'I think he's just scanning the beach for bare tits.'

'If we go out a bit we can face out to sea.'

I rolled off the bed carefully. I've had mishaps with sunbeds before where the whole fucking thing folds in half under you. The sand was hot in the sun. I stood beside her and put my left hand out to her.

'Just to the edge,' she said.

We walked across the sand hand in hand. To our right somebody had done a great job tying coloured wraps together to make a kind of shady tent out of a brolly. There were tyre marks on the beach big enough for a tractor or JCB. Suzi was gripping my hand tightly and holding back as we reached the little bank of seaweed on the edge of the sea, with silvery strands moving in and out on the ripples. I diverted us through a little sandy inlet in the seaweed and walked into the water, half-dragging Suzi like she was a reluctant child.

'I can't do this, Johnny. I really can't.'

In the four years we'd worked together I had never heard her admit to anything she couldn't do. I turned and looked at her – pale but golden in the sunlight. She was actually frightened.

'Tell me,' I said, gently.

She sighed, wrapped her arms around me, and whispered. 'I'm afraid of the sea. I can't swim. Sorry.'

For once, my instincts as a human being trumped my long sojourn in professionalism when it came to Suzi. I pulled her close, hugged her, held her for a long time. Okay, it was probably just a few seconds, but it sure as hell felt like a long time.

I pointed out into the placid sea. 'Look at that kid. How old do think?'

'Four or five.'

'Twenty yards out and only up to his knees.'

She kicked the water, sending spray into the air. 'I feel so fucking stupid.'

You have to take your opportunities when they come. I hugged and hugged her, and then whispered 'Not stupid. I'll teach you to swim. Might take a few days, but in the meantime the only way you're going to drown here is if I hold you under in three feet of water. Trust me.'

She actually kissed me lightly on the lips. 'Just cover,' she said. 'I'm not really kissing you.'

'Of course. Now hold my hand and look like you're enjoying it.'

I led her out into the cool sea very slowly. The beach sloped down a little into a shallow trough under the water and then became shallower again, as though the little waves had managed to scour out a small lagoon. There were just a few wisps of seaweed moving to and fro. A seagull screeched above us. Thin strands of cloud and a vapour trail gleamed in the sky above us. We were here to do a job, but in that moment, I realised that all I really wanted was to be here with Suzi on this beach, in this sea, in this sun, holding her hand. Dangerous.

I waited until the water was just at the top of her thighs and said 'Can you feel the sand between your toes?'

'Yes.'

'Nice?'

'Well. Yes – it's nice.'

'Good. I'm going to kneel down.' As I knelt, the water came up to my chest. I was still holding her hand and looking up to her, the sun bright on her face. 'Do you think you can do that?'

She hesitated, but I knew Suzi could not bear to be seen as a poor weak woman. Her right hand was squeezing mine tightly as she slowly sank until the water covered her breasts and the blue stripe of her bikini top was a blur of colour.

'People do this for fun, Suzi,' I said. 'Here endeth lesson one.'

She wobbled in the water. 'It's hard to stay kneeling,' she said.

'Correct. Your body wants to float. It weighs less. You are a golden fish, really.'

I stood up and pulled her to her feet. 'Look out towards the islands.'

We stood there, facing away from the beach and the man with binoculars.

'I've been thinking,' I said. 'Tourists go everywhere, take pictures of everything. Nobody cares. I think we need to go and see where Tina went last night. And we need to check room twelve in my block. So, after lunch, how about a little drive?'

She splashed me and giggled. 'I was enjoying myself. But you're right. The car's in the car park next to *Waves*. But I'm hungry.'

We rinsed the salt off under the beach shower by the taverna. Suzi wriggled into a light dress and I changed into my dry shorts. *Mistral* was right on the beach – just a few feet up a sandy slope and we were there. There was a pair of long buildings – really just flat wooden roofs on wooden pillars, with tables for two or four. The chairs were simple, with rush seats and some thin cushions. We picked a table right at the end, conveniently placed just under a loudspeaker which was quietly playing a Greek music station.

A short, round man came across, spread a paper cloth across the table, clipped it down, and handed us some menus, then vanished across a little garden with a plastic children's slide and into the building nearer the road, which was higher up. A flight of steps ran up on the left of the building and there was a narrow tar road on the other side between *Mistral* and the next taverna – *Manthos*. It was a busy lunchtime.

'The waiter's called Spiros,' Suzi said, settling her sunglasses on the table.

'Get away!'

'He's still there – the man with the binoculars. The thing is, he's looking out to sea. He's been there a long time, like he's a spotter or something.'

'Keep an eye,' I said. 'I can't get a visual from this angle.'

'Will do.'

Lunch came. Meatballs in a tomato sauce. Fried zucchini. Chips. Bread. Suzi had insisted that we had a small bottle of retsina. I'd never tasted it before we were at the bar on the headland. It was odd, with a savoury under-taste.

'It's pine resin,' she said. 'Brilliant with the

meatballs.'

I wasn't convinced, but I was starting to get a taste for it. There was a speck of white out to sea, coming past one of the islands – a ship of some kind. Suzi put her fork down – she'd eaten her lunch in a few seconds. 'He's gone.'

'What is that? Out there?'

She scrunched her eyes up, put her sunglasses on and stared out to sea. 'Looks like a private yacht. The sort you or I will never own. It's coming from the north, past *Ereikousa*.'

'What's that?'

'Tut, tut. I remember some cocky senior detective saying "No map in your head, you'll end up dead." There are four islands. *Diaplo. Mathraki. Othoni. Ereikousa.*' She pointed to them. '*Ereikousa* is the most north-westerly point in Greece. This beach is facing north. To the north east is Albania. To the north west is Italy. To the south east is mainland Greece. Go north up the Italian coast and eventually you get to Venice. This sea is the Ionian, and it's a part of the Adriatic, which is a part of the Mediterranean. Beyond those islands the sea is very deep.'

'I didn't ask for the whole of fucking Wikipedia, and yes good work, and yes you are insufferably smug.' I paused and said 'How long have you been here?'

'Ten days.'

I thought about it. 'You were here before Maria contacted me. That is astronomically too coincidental to be true. Unless... Maria is working for Intelligence. Is she?'

'Way above my pay scale.'

'Or she's coming at the same thing from a different angle. That's not such a coincidence when you think about it. She part-owns an apartment block here. She has roots here. She gets wind of something going on and she can't ask her sister because she doesn't trust her. She needs to know.'

Suzi leaned across the table and poured the last of the retsina into my glass. 'Johnny,' she said 'There's also a chance that she set you up so they could find out how well their cover was doing. Like a stress test.'

CHAPTER THIRTEEN

We paid our bill and walked across the sand past the Waves taverna to the car parking area. When I saw what she'd got I laughed. A beaten-up Suzuki jeep, probably ten years old, pale yellow, with fading hire-company badges on the doors. The spare tyre on the back was scuffed and didn't inspire much trust.

'You may laugh,' she said, 'but it has a two-point five litre turbo-charged engine, enhanced anti-roll-bars, hardened suspension, and a few other goodies. It looks like shit. Just what a wannabe novelist here on a writing expedition would hire at cut-price.'

'How did you get it?'

'Local cooperation. Shipped over from the mainland on the ferry.'

She pressed her key-fob in a complicated pattern and the doors clicked. 'Very hard to get into if you don't have the codes,' she added. 'Additional heavy-duty locks on the doors. Armoured glass windows. A bit naughty on steep bends at high speed but that just adds to the fun.'

'I don't want fun. Treat me like a nervous old biddy.'

'I usually do.'

'Piss off. Where are we going?'

'Leave it to me.'

I climbed in. The engine started with a low roar – like a lioness with cubs hinting that coming closer would be a serious mistake. We drove toward the stream and then up the little sand-covered road next to *San Stefano Travel*, passing a smart apartment on the left. At the junction with the road by Margarita's supermarket she turned right, heading past *Nafsika* and *Manthos*, up a steady slope and then past a white church.

'That's the church of *Agios Stefanos*,' she said, 'Saint Stephen, in English. I think they only have services on special days.'

We curved to the right around the church, and then the road was flat for maybe a hundred yards before it began to go downwards in a long slope. The headland rose steeply to the left and the road was cut into the side with an embankment on the right, so we couldn't see the sea.

When the road flattened again we were at the harbour. There were cars and trucks parked along the waterfront where fishing boats were tied up. The harbour boom was unusual, a curving strand of piled-up rocks with more boats tied up. Suzi parked opposite a shack with some plastic chairs and tables outside, where a few men were sitting drinking coffee or ouzo and playing backgammon.

As we walked along the harbourside the air was heavy with diesel fumes and a hint of fish. Seagulls circled overhead. There were a couple of fishing boats out of the water, balanced on precarious wooden scaffolds, one of them with a man scraping old paint off. Not a shiny tourist harbour then – an honest working place with working men and no frills.

At the far end, when we reached it, was a rock shelf, hollow underneath where the sea washed in and out in a deep gutter, gurgling and splashing.

'Information,' Suzi said. 'Ferries go every day to the nearby islands – *Mathraki* and *Othoni*. They go to *Ereikousa* from Sidari. The islanders treat them like buses. The small motorboats you can hire on the beach tie up here overnight. The local bus to Corfu Town starts here. It doesn't look much but it's the lifeline for people on the islands. There's not a lot of fish, but better than some parts of the Med. The fishing boats go out in the evening and fish by night with lights. They sell most of their catch to local tavernas. Fish is expensive – but they're up against fish-farms and cold-vans from Corfu Town. Nobody gets rich, but they've been doing it for thousands of years.'

'Thanks,' I said. 'It's a hub.'

'Yes. There is a helicopter pad on *Ereikousa*, but that's it. If you want to get to the islands you have to go by sea, from here or *Sidari*. Oh – and one tip. Don't use the loo.' She pointed to a small square building. 'I'd rather squat in a thorn bush.'

Back in the jeep we drove through the village, turned up the main street past the bakery and *Zorba*'s, up the ever-steeper hill, with a few apartment blocks with swimming pools on the right. She pulled into the car-park in front of a series of low modern buildings with a sign saying *Romanza*.

'This is where Tina parked last night,' she said. 'Great views from up here.'

'She wouldn't be sight-seeing after dark.'

'True. Come and take a look.'

We asked the receptionist if we could have a drink by the pool and went through the building and out onto the terrace. There were white clouds like icing over the top of the Albanian mountains. The entire bay was spread out in vast panorama, the islands so sharp in the clear air that they looked as though they were nearby. A small ferry was crossing the sea, going northwards, a long wake trailing behind it. Suzi had a Coke with lemon slices and I sipped a Mythos.

'Over here,' she said, getting up. I followed her to the far side of the pool. She put her arm around me and whispered 'Look down there.' A path ran in zig-zags down the cliff-side to the beach far below. A man and a woman were climbing slowly up.

'There's a gate at the side of the building,' Suzi said. 'You can use the path without coming through the main bit. This is the last access to the beach. You come out by the place where the nudists hang out, or hang it out.'

'It's bloody steep.'

'Yes, Johnny – but those people are coping and I reckon they could give you thirty years.'

We finished the drinks. I went to the khazi and when I came back Suzi was chatting to the receptionist like they were old friends. Suzi was doing her blonde act – she's good at it.

'Stella says they do Greek nights. D'you fancy that?'

'I thought they did Greek nights every night in Greece.'

Peals of girly laughter. Stella was another attractive woman – the two of them seemed so full of life. Blonde Suzi and brunette Stella. Being smugly girly together. 'Very good, Johnny! It's like food and dancing and a bit of a knees up. You'd love it. Everybody joins in.'

I made a harrumphing sound like a bloke who couldn't think of anything worse than that and I'm sure it sounded genuine because I couldn't really think of anything worse than that. Then I had a vivid image of Andreas in the stream. Definitely worse.

'You don't have to dance,' Stella said, giving me a kindly smile.

'Yes, he bloody does!' Suzi linked her arm in mine. 'He's a good dancer.'

Bollocks I was. Stella passed a card to Suzi, and said 'Just phone up and book. It's very popular.'

We walked back to the Jeep. 'You have multiple personalities,' I said. 'The trouble is I don't much like any of them.'

She slammed the door of the Jeep shut so hard the frame rocked and sat in silence. Silence is a great interview weapon. Nobody likes silence – you can leave people to stew in it until somebody can't bear it any longer. I cracked first.

'You know I don't mean that.'

'Do I?'

I'll probably be banned for public speaking in any institution for saying this, but, fuck it, if a woman gets you on a hook she will let you wriggle until the point of death. The sad truth is that I adored Suzi and did everything I could not to show it. Never once, not ever, had she shown the slightest flicker of anything like it on her side – until that moment in the sea.

'Now where?' I asked. She started the Jeep and revved it. I winced. Wrong sort of attention.

'Stop pulling that face. They'll just think it's got a hole in the exhaust. Half the bloody mopeds have.'

She drove up the last of the hill, then through *Avliotes* village, down its hilly main street, and turned left down a very steep road. At the bottom there was a flat plain with some smart houses and a field with some goats. We turned off this up a side road and she pulled up in a small busy car park in front of a cliff and a smart restaurant called *Seventh Heaven* that was spread out along the cliff top. Touristy, but tasteful.

We walked to the edge of the cliff by a wall and looked down at the winding steps. 'This is the famous *Loggas* Beach,' Suzi said. 'They claim they have the best sunsets. They don't. You can see the sunset all along the west coast and, let's be honest, it's the same sun. Good marketing, though.'

'Are you sure the Jeep's not bugged?'

'Automatic detectors. If there's a bug it won't start and the alarm lights beep a pattern. Perfect excuse to open the bonnet and pretend you're trying to fix it.'

'We have to see what's in room twelve. And we need another tracker on Tina's car.'

'Yes, Boss. Leave the tracker to me. You figure out how to do the room.'

'Don't call me Boss. I'm not.'

'You still think you are. Deep down. Don't you?'

'This is different. We are faffing about with nothing to go on. As far as I'm concerned, we are partners. But we need to get our act together. What is so bloody important here?'

'It has to be something international or the UK wouldn't be involved. As we discussed, it's probably not average crime. That's a job for the local police.'

'Yes – but since the UK left the EU we can't access the EU police alert system. Things have got a lot harder. But Security can do things that the police can't. It's off the radar. Especially if it involves terrorism or crime funding terrorism.'

When I got out of the shower later on there was a text message from Suzi with just a string of digits. I entered them into the scanner program on the laptop. After thirty seconds the spinning wheel cursor went away. There was a satisfying beep, and Google maps appeared with the car marked on it outside *Artemis*. I sent the latest recordings from the bug in Tina's office to Sophia, not because I trusted her, but because I had to stick to routine. Then I texted a reply to Suzi. "Vaso and Yianni's just down the road – 20:45." She sent a smiley back.

We planned it all over supper. She persuaded me to try the *pastitsio* – a local dish of macaroni in a baked cheese sauce with bechamel on top. Got to say it was delicious. The owner's beautiful wife brought us what she said was orange pie. Suzi asked her about it in Greek. I wish the hell I was a linguist.

'It's not what we really call a pie,' said Suzi. 'It's a kind of cake made with ripped-up filo pastry, fresh orange juice and syrup. She has to come in at eight o'clock in the morning to make it.'

'Tell her I think it's heaven.'

'I will.'

'How come you can eat all the food here and stay so slim?'

She smiled. 'Bloody heck, fella,' she said, upping her Yorkshire accent. 'Was that a compliment?'

'Might be.'

'I go for a run every morning at about six. Five miles.'

'Bullshit.'

'How would you know? You've never seen me at six in the morning apart from a night-shift at work.'

'I am painfully aware of that fact, Suzi.'

She demolished the rest of her orange pie – or *portokalopita*, as she called it – and leaned back in her chair. 'You're a funny mixture, Johnny Almond. You're a cocky Londoner with an ego as big as an elephant and at the same time you are painfully shy. Let's have a Metaxa.'

We did. We were sitting on the terrace next to the road, and from time to time a car or a bike went by. We sat in silence for a while, just kind of looking at each other. I couldn't say what I was going to say.

'Work,' I said finally. 'We agree we have to up our public relationship.'

She was trying to suppress a smile. 'Indeed, we do.'

'So, jog up here to me in the morning.'

'Don't be stupid, Johnny. I've got a bag in the car. In that bag is a toothbrush. I draw the line at using yours, okay?'

There was more in the bag than just a toothbrush, it turned out. The first thing she did in my room was open it up and take out what looked like a fountain pen. She clicked the side a few times and an LED lit up white, then green. She went around the room pointing it at skirting boards, under the bed, inside cupboards, behind the curtains. She went into the bathroom and came out not long after holding the bag I'd put in the cistern, and mouthed 'Yours?' I nodded. She shook her head as though I was a kid hiding sweeties.

'All clear,' she said.

'You've got more toys than fucking Hamley's.'

We checked the tracker on Tina's car. She was at

home. Shame. I set an alert to tell us if she moved.

'I guess that's your bed,' she said, pointing to the bedside table with my Kindle Oasis and an ashtray. You couldn't tell from the sheets, which the maid had rendered into things as smooth as cotton snooker tables. 'Don't snore,' she added, 'and don't smoke in bed. If you must smoke, smoke on the balcony.'

She took her bag, went into the bathroom, and I heard her brushing her teeth with what I thought was lethal force but probably meant I was just crap at it. She came out wearing a pink nightdress. I had never in even my most vivid dreams imagined Suzi in a pink nightdress. She didn't do pink. She protested loudly against pink girlie clothes. She railed against the imposition of pink gender markers on young females by the male-dominated fashion industry tycoons. Suzi in pink? About as likely as Boris Johnson in a tutu.

In the bathroom I stripped to my boxers and pretended to do a full dental hygiene job on my mouth, then went back, lay down and pulled the sheet up over me. She peeled the sheet back on her bed and slid in. Then she leaned down and put her hand into the bag beside her bed. She placed a copy of *New Scientist* on the bedside table and a handgun under her pillow.

'What the fuck is that?'

'It's only a SS P365. Nothing special.'

I'd done firearms training. 'It's a nine mill semi-automatic, for Christ's sake.'

'I'm alone with a strange man. You just never know...'

'We are not shooting anybody.'

'Johnny, if I'd had this and come into the building when that arsehole attacked you with a machete I'd have shot him without a second thought. Several times. I kind of like to think you would have done the same if it was me.'

'Of course I bloody would.'

'Well then. Get real. Whoever they are, whatever they're doing, these people are dangerous.'

We lay there glaring at each. Then she reached for her *New Scientist* and made a bit of a show of reading. This wasn't exactly the way I'd hoped escalating our relationship would go.

'Do me one favour,' I said. 'Point it away from me.'

She smiled and repositioned the gun so that the muzzle pointed towards the door. I nodded, and said 'Thanks. Do I get one?'

'Tomorrow. Maybe.'

'What are you reading about?'

'Anomalies in the bottom quark fragmentation data from the Large Hadron Collider.'

'And that means what?'

'It means there could be a fifth force of nature which might just sort out the problems with the standard model of physics.'

I sighed and picked my Kindle Oasis. As always, I rotated it so that I could easily use it with my left hand. My brave but damaged crew were in a submarine in the methane seas of Enceladus with no apparent means of survival. But I couldn't really focus them in my mind with her lying beside me, her blonde hair unleashed and spread out on the pillow.

She put her bedside light off and turned onto her side. The room was dark, the faint light from the Kindle merely showing the curve of her hip under the sheet. I struggled on for maybe twenty minutes and put the Kindle down on my bedside table. Was this what marriage was like? So close and yet so far. A woman who was impossibly lovely – impossibly intelligent – impossibly irritating - and impossibly unobtainable. And a woman with a gun under her pillow.

I slept fitfully, turning over carefully. The sight of Andreas dead in the stream came and went. It was pitch dark in the room. I could have put my Kindle on, but the backlight might have disturbed her.

At just after four I was woken by a soft sound. At first I thought Suzi was snoring, but I realised that she was crying, quietly sobbing into her pillow. Very gently I reached across and put my arm around her. She stopped crying and seemed even to stop breathing. Then her hand found my mine and she squeezed my arm against her stomach.

A very little voice whispered 'I'm frightened.'

'I'm with you,' I whispered.

She squeezed my hand for a while longer as I curled up against her. As we drifted off to sleep my last thought was 'Me too, Suzi. Me too.'

CHAPTER FOURTEEN

She had reverted to normal in the morning. I heard her in the bathroom just after six, and she emerged in shorts, T-shirt and trainers. Before she went for her run she walked around to my side of the bed and gave me an affectionate little kiss on the top of my head. Then she was gone, closing the door quietly behind her. I felt a bit of a slob; I should have gone too, but I knew she'd be over the horizon before I'd made three steps.

I checked under the pillow. The gun was gone. If it was hidden in her bag, I couldn't find it. Whoever had trained her had done a good job.

Cup of tea beside me, I decided to check out the voice recordings. I was getting lazy just sending them to Sophia. Being a detective is like searching pebbles on a beach looking for fossils – unless you pick over them all you could miss the very one. At double-speed playback I could tell which were in English, and those were all talking to residents about buses and pharmacies, the best place to eat, taxis to the airport.

And there it was. A call on her mobile, the voice faint but female. I loaded the file into the Audacity program on the laptop, removed the noise, normalised the sound and then boosted the other side of the call. Lucky me – Tina had put her phone on speaker while she did something else.

Maria: 'Whatever you're doing for them, you have got to stop it, Tina. We could lose everything.'

Tina: 'You know I can't.'

Maria: 'You must. It's dangerous and stupid.'

Tina: 'I'm not stupid.'

Maria: 'Then stop. If you don't, you could die.'

Tina: 'If I stop, you can bet on it. Anyway, I'm busy. Bye.'

Tina cancelled the call and then swore a lot in Greek. Suzi arrived back looking shiny with sweat. I waited until she'd had a shower and played it to her several times, as she insisted.

'Alright,' she said. 'Now we know that Tina is definitely involved in something. Maria knows the broad picture but didn't tell you. We already knew it was dangerous because of Andreas. But that last thing Tina said could mean she's under duress of some kind. When Maria says they could lose everything, what's she talking about? Just this place?'

'We need to get into that room.'

'Yes.'

We took our breakfast down to the pool as the sun rose higher over the eastern hills. A gentle breeze merely put dimples into the water. A perfect day was in the making, but I was unsettled. In an ideal world I would have relaxed and enjoyed the company of this extraordinary woman, all cares left behind at Heathrow, but I felt as though we were playing blindfold chess for very high stakes and not quite able to grasp the pieces on the board. She'd left her hair damp after the shower and as it dried in the warm morning air it started to form little crinkles and just a few tiny curls at the tips. Her ears had small lobes and her eyelashes were surprisingly dark for a blonde. Not mascara. Just a brownish tinge.

*

Tina's car drew up on the road outside. 'Maximum affection time,' I said. Suzi took my damaged hand gently and set it on the table in front of us. She leaned towards me, her fingers brushing mine, gently, tenderly stroking, looking me as though I were the only thing in the world worth looking at. I was obscurely jealous of anybody who had the genuine experience.

Tina didn't break step as she came past, but she gave me a look and a smile that said *I know what you've been doing.* I withdrew my hand and tried to look shy. When we went back up to my room I kept my eyes down, knowing that Tina was watching from the bar as she opened the shutters. Suzi was carrying our mugs and plates, and in my peripheral vision I saw her smile sweetly at Tina, who then said 'You can leave those here, if you like. Zoe will wash them.'

I waited by the entrance door as Suzi dumped the dirty crockery on the bar counter. I heard them introducing themselves and chatting about the lovely morning and what a great supper we'd had last night. Suzi was doing her dumb blonde impression, which was good if you didn't know she could probably run Mensa as a part-time job.

'Brilliant, 'I said as I shut the room door. 'Now all I have to do is spend the rest of the day looking post-coital.'

'You do post-coital well, Johnny. Pre-coital's another question.'

We waited until about ten and doors were banging in the corridors. I took a look outside the room and came back. 'Zoe's doing the first floor,' I said. 'Now would be a good time.'

Every apartment block has a room set aside for all the gubbins the cleaners needed – mops, buckets, detergents, bags, clean sheets and towels. And keys. In *Artemis* that was where room eleven should have been, on my floor, at the other end of the corridor. I waited until I heard Suzi talking to the maid in Greek and English, probably asking pointless touristy questions and questions about children and maybe grandchildren. I'd seen her in action. She was very good at it – such a sweet young copper out to do good in the world – butter wouldn't melt – the daughter every mum and dad would want. She had one task: hold the maid up for as long as possible.

The door of the maid's room was ajar. I slipped in quietly and quickly and searched around on the walls. In the corner was a wooden board with cup hooks on it with spare keys dangling from them. I grabbed the key for room twelve and moved the key from room four onto that hook to avoid attention. Carefully out of eleven and into twelve, closing the door behind me.

The beds were stripped, their mattresses standing on edge, presumably to keep them aired. The room smelled stale, unused, no hint of after-sun and coconut sun cream.

There were only two unusual items: on the table there was something electronic, high-tech looking with twin joysticks like a games console controller, only bigger. Next to it was a charger with a mains plug. On the floor by the table was a black hold-all. I unzipped it quickly and looked inside, but it was empty. I took some pictures with my phone, and I was just going to leave the room when I heard voices in the corridor. My phone beeped – a text from Suzi saying "Hide now." Clearly, through the door, I heard Tina's voice talking loudly to the maid in the corridor. Shit.

I stuck a bug on the air-conditioning unit, ran across to the window, undid the glass doors and the shutters, went through, pulled the glass doors firmly shut and then the shutters, trying to make it look as though they were locked. I was on the balcony. There was nowhere to hide here, but I kept in a low crouch so I couldn't be seen from the pool, which was now as crowded as it got. I sat in a corner and waited, glad that the balcony didn't have a trendy glass wall or railings. I suddenly felt a desperate urge for a pee – nerves, I told myself, because I hadn't been in action like this for a long time. You don't need a piss. You can tell your body a lot of things, but it's about as obedient as a wild horse. Eventually, I gave in, and pissed into the wall near a little drain to let the rainwater out. Slowly, slowly – hold it in a bit. Don't make it rain down below.

My phone beeped again. Suzi: "Clear."

I crouch-walked to the shutters and pulled them open. But the glass doors were the sort that jammed if you pulled them too hard, which was basically crap design.

I phoned Suzi. 'What the fuck happened?'

'Tina came up. I couldn't keep them for long.'

'I'm stuck on the balcony of number twelve. The bloody door's jammed.'

'Have you got the key? If you drop it I'll come and get you. Wait until I say.'

I went back to my corner and leaned against the wall. Music played, people splashed and called below. Then I peeped over the edge. Suzi wandered beside the pool as though deciding whether to swim and sat down at a table. She tapped at her phone, and mine rang.

'Can't do. Too many people you might hit.'

Think fast, Johnny.

'How many rooms can you see?'

'If I move down I can see them all.'

'Do it.'

I knew room eleven didn't have any residents, because it was the maid's room. That left five rooms between this and mine. The balconies had a four-foot partition wall between them, and on top of that was a privacy screen, horizontal at first, then tapering down to a foot before the front wall.

I crawled along and grabbed a white plastic chair from beside the white plastic table. I put the chair in the corner next to the partition wall. Peering out over the pool, just my eyes above the front wall, I scanned the pool-siders. Nobody was looking this way.

The chair was flimsy and trembled as I climbed onto it. With one last scan of the pool I eased over the last few inches of the wall and dropped into the balcony of room eleven. My hand hurt. I had to use the palm of my hand and try not to grasp concrete from now on. It looked like an assault course of the sort they give you when you're training. Climb over that lot if you can, you useless dick.

There were people on the balcony of room ten, arguing over a crossword puzzle, and whether he drank too much, the weather forecast, whether there was too much meat on the menus in the village, should they take their blow-up ring to the beach or not bother, why he hadn't made his bed, had he been too rude with somebody last night, was that his fourth cigarette in the last hour. But even they would have noticed if I climbed across their balcony.

They were labouring over the last clue - twenty-seven across. She read it out increasingly loudly three times. 'Exist – after – dark – sir, he heard.' They argued about it for ages, getting nowhere. Back in the old days at the end of a night shift Suzi and I sometimes had a fried breakfast in a Turkish café near the Station. Or, to be more accurate, she had yoghurt and fruit while I stuffed eggs and bacon down. She always bought The Guardian in the paper shop next door and subjected me to the cryptic crosswords, which were lethally difficult. I reckon she was the only Guardian reader in the Stokey nick, which was more Daily Mail territory. Suzi had a mission to teach me how to do the fucking crossword. Now, I'm not utterly stupid. I can tell a hawk from a handsaw and know it was Hamlet. I nearly went to Uni to do English but decided I was too lazy. So, I looked at the first and last word of the clue because one of those was probably the actually meaning, and guessed. She hated it when I was right. That was not the way you were supposed to do these things. She insisted I went through the painful process of explaining *why* it fitted with all the other bits of the clue even though I explained over and over again that I wasn't being paid by GCHQ, and it was supposed to be fun, for Christ's sake.

After ten minutes of listening to futile ramblings from the other side of the wall I'd had enough. The longer I stayed here the greater the chance of the maid coming out to sweep the balcony or take a breather. I cupped my hands around my mouth to make the sound as directionless as possible and shouted 'Benighted!'

There was a pause. He shouted 'Thanks' and said to her 'That's right, isn't it? Be is exist, after dark is night, he is a Sir and night sounds like knight.'

'We should have got that,' she said. 'It's obvious.' Yes, love – they're always obvious when you get the answer. Apart from the ones where it wasn't the slightest bit obvious, because the setter was a pretentious wanker.

'Pool or beach?' he asked again.

They twittered away as they went inside. I risked peeping around the plastic separator between the balconies towards my room, and it wasn't good news. There were couples on the balconies of the next two rooms. Why, God only knew. Why did some people fly over a thousand miles to somewhere with a mile-long sandy beach and spend their entire holiday beside a swimming pool? Eventually I heard their door slam, and climbed over the wall as discreetly as I could.

Their room was a thing of contrasts: make-up and sun stuff neatly arranged on the dressing-table area, a smoothed sheet, a ruffled sheet, mugs and plates washed and drying in the rack by the cooker. And a half-open suitcase with clothes hanging out and a trail of electrical leads beside the wall socket. Hers and his. I felt a moment of solidarity with the poor bastard.

I peered round the door. The corridor was empty, and I pushed the keys to room twelve hard under the door of room eleven before I went downstairs and out beside the pool, hoping the maid would think she, or more likely Tina, had dropped them. Job done.

Suzi had moved a sun-bed around a bit so that

she could lie on it and see the apartment without turning her head unnaturally. She was wearing a blue bikini with gold stars on it that looked suspiciously like the EU flag, and sunglasses.

I sat down on the bed next to hers. 'Did you really have a bikini with you?' I said. 'Your bag's like the fucking Tardis.'

'Girls have bags with them and clean knickers. Men have neither, in my experience. I couldn't call you because I could see you had neighbours. Why are you wincing?'

I held my right hand out a little. It was red and swollen, and the scars were standing out. 'It's okay,' I said.

'Bollocks. That needs attention.'

CHAPTER FIFTEEN

Despite my protestations we set off down the road and up the main street, past *Barras* and *Thomas Bay*, up a bit more past *Bar 38* and a car and bike rental outfit. There was an open patch of land with a couple of cars parked on it and alongside that a low building with a table and a couple of chairs outside. A sign in English said "Clinic."

The nurse, whose name it turned out was Dora, was smiling and efficient. She examined my hand and asked 'You had operation?'

'Yes. I fell on it this morning.'

'Is painful?'

I shrugged. Suzi spoke to Dora in rapid Greek and Dora laughed. 'I think I call the doctor. Come in here.'

We all went into an examination room with a bed. Dora clipped an oximeter on my left index finger, looked at the red LED "97" and said 'Okay. You wait outside until doctor comes.'

We sat in the shade of a brolly for a few minutes. It was very warm. Suzi got up and said 'Stay there and don't bloody move or I'll stamp on your hand. Got it?' I nodded. She walked away and came back five minutes later with two bottles of Coke and bag of oregano crisps.

I passed her my phone. 'What's that?' She studied the photos from room twelve intently, then transferred them to her phone and passed mine back to me. She tapped various icons on her phone and waited until the results came back.

'As I thought,' she said. 'It's a top-range controller for a drone. Expensive. Nice bit of kit.'

'There was no drone,' I said. 'What the hell does she need a drone controller for?'

'There's only one thing you can do with a drone controller and that's fly a drone. From which I draw the inevitable conclusion that the drone is somewhere else.'

'All they do is take pretty pictures, right?'

'Wrong. A top-notch drone will cost you over ten thousand pounds and carry over two kilos of payload. Want to see some?'

'No.'

She said 'Tough,' and played with her phone. I sat back and swallowed what were left of the crisps, took a few drinks of cold fizzy Coke from the plastic bottle. A grey Audi pulled into the parking area. The driver was a balding guy who merely got out and leaned on the bonnet. The passenger was a woman in her fifties – what you might call a dark shade of blonde. She took a medical bag from the back seat of the car and pulled on a white lab-coat and a surgical mask. She went inside the building and a minute or two later Dora came out and said 'Doctor will see you now.'

Doctors love my hand. They examine it like it was a rare find from an Egyptian tomb. 'You had a cut?' she said. I agreed. 'It was a good operation. No tearing from your fall. It's a bit angry. Keep it out of the sun. I will give you some antibiotics and anti-histamines. Take all of them. That is important. Do not drink excessive alcohol. Better to drink none.'

I was about to debate the finer points of what "excessive" meant when Suzi coughed and gave me one of those looks.

'Yes, doctor,' I said submissively. 'Thank you.'

She reached into her bag and passed me two strips of pills. 'One a day for five days,' she said. 'You pay Dora.' With that she just half-smiled and walked out.

Dora wrote me a bill and took my insurance details. No cards. I handed over a couple of fifty euro notes and got a ten back. I swallowed an antibiotic and an antihistamine with some Coke.

We walked through the village until just past the paper shop and turned up a steep slope – maybe thirty yards or so. The path divided beside a little shrine with an icon inside a glass door. One path went left behind *The Little Prince*, one continued up the hillside to some villas. Suzi turned right down a slope and then left, zig-zagging between bungalows until we came to one in its own patch of grass with high walls on three sides. A couple of sunbeds half-folded were on the patio, and there was a brick-built barbecue. It was shady and cool, with the afternoon sun hidden behind a high flank of the hill to the west.

Suzi thumbed her phone and studied the screen. 'All clear,' she said. 'Come on.' We went inside to a nice dining area, a kitchen and two bedrooms. Her laptop was on the dining table.

'How's the novel coming along?' I asked her.

'Slowly, as it should. People come here to write and then spend most of their day sitting by the pool reading other people's novels.'

'You haven't got a pool,' I said.

'No,' she answered. 'Perfect, isn't it?' She laughed and added 'I get regular downloads of bits of the novel.'

'You bloody cheat. Somebody else is writing it.'

'They are not paying me to write "War and Peace". Just to prevent the former and keep the latter.'

'What's it about?'

'You wouldn't like it.'

''Why not?'

'It used to be called Chick Lit until that was deemed unfeminist. Clothes, girly chat, handsome useless men, soft porn. Stuff you wouldn't know about.'

'I can do the handsome bit - and the porn bit.'

'Johnny, you're a potentially lovely man hiding inside an arsehole. You are acceptably good-looking. You are not a wealthy financier with a yacht and a thousand quid suit. You are absolutely not a pin-up. You are not novel material. Sorry.' A pause, and she said 'Actually, I take that back - at the moment you might just make it into Frankenstein.'

'What as?'

'A failed prototype?'

I put my good hand out, meaning to poke her in the stomach, but she grabbed it, held it up to her mouth and bit my fingers. Hard. I managed to wrench it away. 'Ouch! Why did you do that?'

'I like biting. You're the nearest flesh. Now – let's get back to work.'

In the movies you see hackers typing at high speed, pages of obscure numbers rolling up the screen, lights blinking. Crap. It took her nearly an hour of painstaking work. Typing a command, waiting for the result, swearing, rubbing her eyes. 'Right,' she said. 'Test.'

Our phones pinged at exactly the same time. When I opened the text message there was an embedded image of a dark room.

She stood up and stretched. 'Your laptop looks as though it's off, but it isn't. It's waiting for a signal from the bug a few rooms away from it. The bug's smart and when it detects movement or light change in room twelve your laptop will signal this laptop, which will send SMS messages to our phones. I hope.'

'It just did. Brilliant.'

It was gone four in the afternoon and we hadn't eaten anything. I had the basics in a bag I'd packed before we went to the clinic, so I stuffed my Speedo shorts and a towel into a plastic carrier bag that was in the kitchen and we made our way down to the beach for a beer and a snack. The light was beautiful: mellow gold sparkling on the little ripples at the edge of the sea. We parked our bags on

JIM HAWKINS

a couple of sunbeds in front of the *Waves* taverna. Where *Mistral* was mostly a garden with wooden shelters, *Waves* was a brick building with a shady terrace under a sloping roof.

We shared some kalamari with tzatziki and pitta bread while I sipped a Mythos and Suzi had a glass of dry white wine. The antibiotics and antihistamines were kicking in and my hand had stopped hurting. We changed in the lavatories and walked over the hot sand to the sea. I made her lie down and dip her face in the water. When I say "made" I am editing out several minutes of tantrums. I knew that she'd do it eventually out of sheer bloody refusal to let me think she was weak. One thing I learned in the Met was that phobia is upside-down addiction. It's addiction to not doing something. After a couple of squealing attempts she started enjoying it and allowed herself to roll around near the edge of the water. One nil to the Arsenal. I rolled around beside her because standing up and looking dominant would not have helped.

I couldn't help but notice that her nipples were hard under her bikini top in the cool water but I tried to put it out of my mind. For now, at least. Twenty yards away a toddler was screaming with delight as his father splashed water on his back, and I felt as though we were children like that. And I felt sad and happy at the same time – sad that we were two lonely people here for something totally other than this – and joy that we had the space to roll in the edge of the sea and pretend that it wasn't happening. We moved a little further out in the hollow before the first low sandbank and I persuaded her to lie on her stomach and support herself on her arms in the arm-deep water as the rest of her body floated free.

'Now,' I said. 'Just lift your hands off the sand for a few seconds. The sand's always there. You're safe. And remember, it doesn't matter if you get your face wet.' She flailed around for a few moments and then got the hang of it. Her face lit up with a broad beam. I taught her how to kick her legs and go with the water, not against it. I held her hand as she floated on her back.

She stood up and said 'I'm going to do it, aren't I?' And she put her arms around me and kissed me on the lips. As in really kissed me, holding me close.

I was, of course, shooting myself in the foot. This was the only weakness I'd found in this enigmatic woman from somewhere vaguely up north, the only tiny bit of power I had, and I was teaching her how to overcome it. But that kiss! If I remember nothing else I will remember just how alive I felt when her lips touched mine.

We made our way up from the beach. We were near the *Beachcombers* restaurant, so we went in and booked a table for eight-thirty. At her little villa there were no alerts and nothing unusual on the trackers, and I left, reluctantly, and walked the few hundred yards to *Artemis*.

Tina was shutting the pool bar, but she waved me over.

'You're a dark horse, aren't you?'

I shrugged. 'Right place, right time. Know what I mean?'

She laughed.

'It's not against the house rules, is it? She won't steal the china,' I said.

'Of course not. I like our guests to have a good time. Classy-looking lady, though. What does she do?'

Fucked if I know why I said it, but 'She's an embalmer, or something like that. Not sure what it is. You'll have to ask her.'

She nearly dropped the bottles she was holding. 'Embalmers do things with dead people. Are you sure that's what she does?'

'She's brought me back to life!' I said, and added 'Got you there, Tina. She's writing a novel – that's what she's really doing. At least that's what she says she's doing. How would I know?'

'I'd love to talk to her. I've always wanted to write, but I never have time. Life gets in the way.'

She was right. Life gets in the way of everything – mostly life. But I sensed an opportunity here – a way to get under Tina's guard. She didn't strike me as the type who would fly a drone for the fun of it, and anyway, where was the drone? Those things go together, don't they? Drone and controller – both useless without the other. But if Suzi could become best mates with Tina she might get some hints.

What we really needed to know was whether Tina was innocent, or involved in some minor criminal activity, or involved in something of interest to the security forces. And whether she was doing whatever it was voluntarily or under duress. Was she involved in the murder of Andreas? Somehow, I didn't think so, but I'd been a detective long enough to know that looking good and speaking nicely does not stop you being totally evil.

Maybe it was because I'm a bloke and Tina was very attractive, but I really wanted her to be innocent.

*

There was a chalk-board lit up outside *Beachcombers* advertising fresh mussels every day. We sat out on the balcony area under the flat-roofed cover about ten feet above the beach. Suzi has this effortless way of finding out who's called what so it turned out the smiling woman who took out orders was English and called Sue. Her husband was Kimon, the plump Greek man sitting behind the till inside the very smart restaurant. The big black dog ambling about wasn't theirs but had adopted them the way dogs do.

This place didn't pretend to be a Greek taverna. It was a Mediterranean bistro. It didn't do wine in a jug. I love mussels. Don't ask me why – I just do. I'm not a big eater, really. I don't measure meals by their size. Give me good – and just enough of it. The problem with mussels is that they're a two-handed event and my right hand wasn't even up to its pathetic best.

Suzi came to the rescue, quickly stripping the mussels out of their shells, chucking the shells into the bowl beside me and leaving the flesh in the winey soup. Fresh, hand-made, chips were easy. Garlic bread was easy. Sipping the fresh, cold, flower-scented bottle of house white was easy. Eating the mussels with a spoon was easy.

The sun was down but the afterglow lit up the sky. Suzi was wearing a calf-length dark navy-blue dress and she'd slung a black cardigan on against the cool of the evening air. I was wearing jeans and a bottle-green hoodie. As darkness fell we could see the lights of *Mistral* below us to the left along the beach, and *Waves* to our right. Far out in the sea a ship's light passed from time to time between us and the distant islands.

I briefed her on the chat I'd had with Tina. 'You'd better bone up on actually being a writer,' I said. 'She wants advice, and having a ghost-writer doesn't really do it.'

'The thing is, Johnny,' she said, 'I am writing a novel. One hour a day.'

I sipped some wine. 'Two questions. Why did you lie, and what's it called?'

'Why did I lie? Because I felt like it. What's it called? I keep changing it. Today it's called "Learning to swim."'

At which point both our phones beeped and vibrated on the table.

CHAPTER SIXTEEN

The images relayed from the bug showed Tina picking up the bag, putting the controller in and going. The tracker on her car traced her route through the village and up the hill. She parked at *Romanza* just like she had before.

We could never drive there in time, even in Suzi's hot-rod. I dumped some euros on the table and waved to Sue. There were steps leading down to the beach, and we took them fast. The black dog thought this was exciting and came loping down with us. It was dark as we sprinted along the beach and splashed across the stream.

We ran between sun-beds in the faint glow of lights from the hotels and cafés beside us. Suzi was well ahead of me by the time we reached the nudist zone and the dog was running between us, sometimes splashing into the water at the edge of the sea and zig-zagging. I was worried about one of us tripping over him. He was having a good time and plainly didn't give a shit.

By the time we got to the bottom of the path leading up to *Romanza* I was completely knackered and panting, trying hard to supress it. I ran into the back of Suzi. She grabbed me and whispered 'Shush' into my ear. Faint shadows moved up the steep path.

I could hear Greek music from above and a cross

between a whine and a hum going out to sea. The dog barked at the figures on the path and they stopped. Suzi grabbed me and held me in a kiss.

'People come out here for a shag in the sand,' she whispered. 'Pretend we're having sex.'

In moments of stress irrelevant things run through the mind, like, for example, the hours I'd spent on my own pretending we were locked in a passionate embrace. We lay down on the hard sand, wrapped up together. The dog came and inspected us, decided we were boring, and ran off towards the sea.

'Shall we follow?' asked Suzi.

'I don't think so. We won't catch them and it's too exposed.'

We stood up and the dog rushed back and shook water and sand over us. Why the fuck wasn't he asleep? Doggies weren't supposed to be up and about at midnight, were they? Way out to sea the lights of a big ship passed towards the south. The breeze was kicking up a bit and the air was cool. We started walking back along the beach.

'I'm pretty sure the drone went out to sea,' I said. 'But they're not waiting for it to come back. Personally, I wouldn't just send God knows how many thousand quids'-worth of drone out over the water and just bugger off.'

'Which means,' Suzi said 'it's going to land somewhere else. Under somebody else's control.'

'Is that possible? I thought those things were kind of wedded to a controller – otherwise it would be chaos.'

'I'll check later.'

'How long did you say those things can fly for on one charge?'

'Just under an hour for the serious ones, I think.'

'Is that time to get to the islands, d'you think?'

'Easily, on a one-way trip. Doubt if you'd get there and back though.'

'Why do you say that?'

'I was thinking. You said there wasn't a drone in that room in *Artemis,* and Tina didn't have a drone on tonight's images from the bug. That's odd. The drone was somewhere else. So, what if they were just meeting the drone and then sending it back again?'

'I like it. It has to be smuggling. The drone flies in. They land it and get whatever it is, then send it back again. It's small – it's under the radar.'

We'd reached the point where the cliffs became lower as we reached the valley and there was plenty of light for our night-adjusted eyes from the buildings along the waterfront. The dog loped in circles from us to the beach and back as though he wanted us to go for a swim.

I stopped. Suzi carried on for a few yards, then slowed and came back. 'What?' she said. I pointed out to sea, where the lights of the boat were moving faster now towards the south. It was hard to judge the distance but my impression was that it was further out than it had been.

'Twenty minutes each way. Ship to shore, shore

to ship.'

'Complicated operation. It would have to be a high-value cargo, Johnny.'

We walked on. 'Street price of heroin is what? Twenty thousand quid a kilo? Two kilos a trip? That's serious money.'

Suzi looped her arm through mine. 'Clever clogs,' she said. 'I'll drop you off. Got to make a few calls.'

Before I went to bed I made a cuppa and checked-out the laptop. Tina's car had driven from *Romanza* down the hill and into the village. She's turned off the main road to the left and parked for seven minutes, then come out and back up the hill and home. I had a look at the area on Google maps and planned for tomorrow. I slept very well – the run along the beach had completely knackered me. I'd only managed about two pages on my Kindle before my eyes refused to stay open any longer.

*

It was another sunny morning in the last days of May. Small birds were twittering as they flew back and forth from mud nests stuck under over-hanging beams or perched in neat rows on the overhead power lines. As I walked into the village a van came down the road very slowly with its tail-gate open; it was loaded with vegetables and a very loud stream of Greek from a looped tape shouted an unintelligible list of presumably spuds, onions and other essentials for your five a day. I liked it in a masochistic way because it really felt as though I was somewhere far away from the streets of north London. If the guy had tried it back home some plod would've nicked him for breach of noise abatement rules or dangerous driving or littering if a carrot fell out. Being a miserable bastard comes with the job, and there are those who enjoy that role. After a couple of years in CID and a few post-mortems you stopped bothering about most things that weren't totally evil because from time to time that's what you had to deal with. A loud-hailer and some beans does not rank with the rape of a four-year-old and a pathetic small body dumped in some bushes.

The smell of fresh bread was overwhelming as I walked past the bakery, past the surgery, remembered I hadn't taken my antibiotics, and carried on in front of *Silver Moon* apartments. There was a small road alongside it, and I knew from the tracker that was where Tina had gone last night. People around the *Silver Moon* pool glanced at me as I walked by and went back to their Jeffrey Archer novels. There wasn't anything interesting about me. I wasn't a giant or a dwarf. I was depressingly average in all dimensions with boring mid-brown hair and unexceptional features. I was a bloke walking along a road. Totally unmemorable – which happens to be an asset for a detective: please don't see me, please don't remember me – I am just background noise. Until I catch you slapping a sixteen-year-old Latvian girl you've trafficked and then you'll remember the pain as I wrench your arm up your back with slightly more than recommended force and grind your nose into the dirt. Even then you won't remember me. You'll remember the unsmiling face of the Custody Sergeant and the smell of vomit in the corridor on the way to your cell. You'll remember losing your belt and shoe-laces and the scarcely-disguised look of disgust on the face of the over-worked duty solicitor who will ensure that everything's done by the book. You probably won't even remember Suzi because she works hard at looking anonymous when she's on duty. You certainly won't imagine she was the one who kicked you behind the knee when you wouldn't go down. Your complaints will be noted and ignored.

The sun was in my face as I walked along the narrow road looking for tyre marks in the dust. Soon there was a metal fence on my left. The road curved to the left and I could see a big building which looked dilapidated and weary. My thought was that it was a failed hotel of some sort. It was long, with narrow rooms on the first floor and a flat roof. Some of the shutters were hanging askew and the weeds on the land around it were high and dotted with tiny pink flowers. The road was pitted with potholes and straggly grass grew in patches. It looked as though it could have been imposing in its heyday.

The fence continued as I rounded the curve in the track – seven feet high with barbed wire running along the top. Where the track culminated in a car-park area there was a tall barred metal gate and a sign saying "Private No Entry" in English with Greek underneath. There were two well-oiled heavy-duty padlocks on the gate – shiny and definitely recently put there. There were tyre marks in the dust and leaves on the car park, as though a car had turned here. The breeze was strong enough to blow stuff about and it was obvious that tyre marks wouldn't last long. I took some pictures of the treads in the dirt, wishing I could call in SOCO to take some plaster casts. More enlightened forces than the Met changed the name from "Scenes of Crime Officers" to "Scientific Investigation Units" or similar things years ago to avoid the politically-incorrect implication that there had been a crime when it might only have been an alleged crime. Who cares? Anyway, computers could do magic with a photograph these days.

I was snapping away with my phone at the gate when thought I caught a flash of movement on the roof of the derelict building, but it could have been anything and I wasn't bothered because tourists will take pictures of anything. But to be on the safe side I turned and took a few more of the view away from the house, lit a cigarette and strolled away as though I hadn't got a care in the world, which wasn't true because the Gooners were playing Liverpool that night and losing to them was only just down the disaster scale from losing to Spurs or the Man U filth.

Tina's car was parked outside *Artemis* when I got

back, nicely hidden from the pool bar by the incline and the wall, and I quickly took a picture of the tyres before I sauntered up the steps swinging a blue carrier bag in my left hand. Suzi was perched on a bar stool drinking coffee and talking in an animated way to Tina, who was laughing. They looked like they were old friends.

I walked up to them and dumped the carrier bag on the bar counter.

'Morning ladies' I said. 'Apple pie, cakes, croissants. Any chance of a cup of tea, Tina?' She did stuff with a mug and hot water.

Suzi was working hard at the girlie thing. 'Did you really tell Tina I was an embalmer?'

'Well, you certainly put some life into me.'

Tina smiled across the bar. 'Ooh, you charmer!'

I smiled modestly. I think it was modestly. Never been much good at it. 'Nobody's ever said that to me before.'

'I believe you,' said Suzi, turning to Tina for solidarity. I liked to think it was just professionalism, but I had my doubts. She could use the truth like a knife to get under the skin of a suspect. Male and suspect go together.

'What have you got planned for tonight, Johnny?' Tina asked.

'Nothing much. Wouldn't mind watching Arsenal v Liverpool at nine o'clock.'

Suzi made an exaggerated yawn, and Tina said 'Perfect. You do that. I'm having a girls' night out with a couple of friends and I thought Suzi might like to come along. If you don't mind?'

I feigned a moment of reluctance, as though I was giving up something precious, then accepted the inevitable. 'Brilliant!', I said, and then to Suzi, 'Maybe we could hook up later?'

Suzi smiled coyly. 'Maybe. Let's see how it goes.'

Perfectly done. Shags are conditional, little boy, and totally under my control. Which was so true it was more painful than a blade in your hand. They had become a team. I was third division, useful for goal practice, utterly dispensable. She and Tina had me squirming under their thumbs and she had bloody-well taken over the initiative. All I could do was to open the carrier bag and reveal the goodies. They were, of course, very grateful as they munched apple pie. Well done, Suzi. You should have stayed in the Met and taken over. God help us.

We chatted about the weather and nothing very significant for half an hour. Tina said Suzi had been very helpful about writing and I said I was pleased and what the fuck did I know about it.

'Talking of which,' said Suzi, 'I need to do some! See you later guys. Johnny – one thirty on the beach.' She pecked me on the cheek in a proprietorial way and walked off down the path. We watched her go.

'She's a bit special,' Tina said.' 'Are you going to see her after you get back?'

'Up to her.'

'Don't be such a wimp, Johnny. She really likes you. Go for it.'

'I don't want to overdo it.'

Tina sighed. 'Faint heart never won fair maiden. Word of advice. Be a bit stronger – she's a strong woman. She wants you to be strong too.'

I held my hands out. 'Que sera sera,' I said.

She shook her head. 'Sera will be what you want sera to be.'

CHAPTER SEVENTEEN

Back upstairs I phoned Tariq with a few more requests. I really wished he could be part of our little team. That way I wouldn't be needing to buy the entire output of the Talisker whisky distillery when I got back home. I was feeling optimistic because if we could find out what was coming in or out on the drone it would be job done. Then I could decide whether to stay with Security or go back to a more comfortable job lurking about furtive fucks and jealous spouses, most of whom didn't give a toss about the sex but wanted the money.

I downloaded the image processing program Tariq suggested but, to be fair, he did say if that wasn't good enough he had some pretty powerful stuff that he couldn't give me. You may well ask why I didn't just send it via Suzi to GCHQ or wherever. Call me paranoid, but I couldn't see the landscape of what we were involved in and I didn't know whom to trust. Apart from Suzi – and she'd lied to me systematically for several years. All the same, I still believed I could trust her, which was almost certainly stupid, but, you know, instinct and those long nights in cars visiting stabbings and drinking coffee from cardboard cups by the side of the road when anybody sensible would have been tucked up with somebody at least tolerable or an uncomplaining teddy-bear.

The tyre marks definitely matched. We could place Tina at the top of the path by *Romanza* and at the abandoned building last night. I ran the image-enhancement program and loaded some pictures of the derelict hotel. Step by step I pulled a rect-angle around an area of the picture on the roof and hit the Enhance button. And there he was – too blurred to recognise but maybe holding a cam-era with a telephoto lens, his arms up to steady it. He was wearing a black shirt with something on it that the software couldn't resolve. I'd reached the limit of what I could do, and emailed the picture to Tariq. I knew he'd understand my shorthand when I merely said "Man on the roof." He replied "Busy. Get back to you later."

I couldn't hang around here too long or it would look suspicious, so I stuck the laptop into my ruck-sack along with my beach gear, pulled my incred-ibly tasteful Arsenal baseball cap onto my head, fit-ted my polarised shades on and went out into the sun beside the pool and along the path. Alan was on his way back to the bar to stock up on lager. 'How did you pull that blonde then, you jammy bugger,' he said in that friendly bantering way that suggested he should have been first in line. Bloody hell, I wasn't even sure *I* was first in line, and the idea that there was a line didn't cheer me up at all. Suzi was many things, but she sure as hell wasn't a one-night-stand. What we had was abond that comes from ploughing through a tidal wave of the painful shit that people inflict on each other day after day, and keeping each other going. We didn't rescue kittens from trees or call in the transporter to shift a car some tosspot had parked on a zebra crossing. When CID was called in some serious crap had happened or was about to happen. It's not a nice job. Most of the time we were on a hiding to nothing, and we knew it, which breeds a kind of darkness in the heart that can get to you if you let it. If you watch TV you see criminals doing stupid things that get them nicked. It does happen. Stupid criminals do get nicked, and it helps the crimes solved statistics. But successful criminals are very, very bright and sometimes have more resources than we do. Plus the fact that only the dim ones do paperwork and we consumed a Norwegian forest every other day with a pointless snail-trail of tick-boxes and forms.

You'd have thought she'd had enough of that, but when I got to *Mistral* she was sitting in a shady corner writing in a hard-back book. I mean – with a pen! Who did that these days? I padded up quietly behind her all ready to say Boo. Her elbow swung back and hit me in the midriff. Hard. I collapsed into the nearest chair.

'That fucking hurt,' I gasped.

'I fucking hope so. Be thankful I didn't do it harder.'

Spiros had seen this and laughed, then walked briskly inside the building and came out with a life-saving beer and a cold glass. Suzi closed her writing book before I could see what she was writing.

'You are such a bitch,' I said, trying hard not to gasp.

'Diddums. You taught me how to keep alert using peripheral vision. And if you want to creep up on people I suggest not wearing yellow shorts and an orange T-shirt. It's not on the SAS approved camouflage list.'

'Consider me suitably humiliated. You're a good typist. Why are you writing by hand?'

'I'm an old-fashioned girl. I like the feel of a pen on paper. And the fact that paper doesn't crash and lose what you've been writing. Add to that the fact that it's shorthand. My own shorthand, not Pittman's, so it's totally unintelligible to anybody but me.'

'I bet GCHQ or the CIA or the FSB could do it.'

'Probably. But they'd waste a lot of time until they found out it was just a novel.'

'*Learning to Swim*.'

'That was yesterday's title. Today it's called *I always knew he was a dickhead*.'

The Mythos tasted good. Just the right blend of lightness and body in the warm air. The pain in my stomach was easing away. Below, on the beach, there was a mixture of semi-permanent straw-topped parasols and white canvas brollies rippling in the southerly breeze as small power boats with sunshades criss-crossed in the turquoise sea. The islands were hazy and distant. People were relaxing over their lunch along the tables. Sue walked down the stairs from *Beachcombers* wearing a black swimsuit, with the black dog lolloping along behind her and they both went into the water.

'Nice life,' I said, pointing them out to Suzi. 'Open your restaurant in the evening. Get the prep done in the day and go to the beach. Perfect.'

'You'd get bored,' she said. 'You're not good at doing boring. Although – come to think of it...'

'Enough. Can you get my laptop out?'

She undid the straps on my rucksack and pulled out the computer. I turned it on and logged in.

'There's no Wi-Fi here,' I said, 'so I took some screenies of *Marinetraffic.com*.'

The first picture showed a map of our area and the islands, with little boat icons. I pointed to one between *Agios Stefanos* and *Othoni*. 'That's last night when we were up the beach. And this,' I said as I flicked to a second picture, 'is the previous time Tina took a jaunt up the hill to *Romanza* and no doubt down the cliff path. Same boat.'

I flicked to a picture of the details of the boat. It was an expensive luxury cruiser of the sort that plutocratic football-club owners liked to pootle about in. It was registered in Albania and called *Lirinë* – which Google helpfully informed me was the Albanian for "freedom."

Suzi grabbed her phone and relayed this information to somebody very quickly. Almost at the same time my phone tweeted the arrival of a text message. It was from Tariq, with a picture attached. My picture of the man on the roof run through the Met's latest state-of-the-art image enhancement software. When Suzi hung up her call I held my phone out to her.

He was tall and well-built, shaven-headed, maybe in his mid-fifties, sun-tanned or olive skin.

'Organised crime muscle,' said Suzi. In other words, an enforcer for a bunch of not very nice-to-know crooks. We'd seen plenty of them. They're hard to put down unless you can aim a lot of guns at them. He could have been a carbon copy of the man who attacked me with the machete. That day, I did not have a lot of guns.

The sign on his T-shirt was odd and unfamiliar – a capital A where the right leg was an elongated zigzag with an arrow point at the end. 'What the fuck is that?' I asked.

'Looks like a Heavy Metal band,' said Suzi. 'You know, death, lightning, the Apocalypse. All that bollocks.'

My phone chirped again. Tariq: *Before you ask again it's an international neo-fascist neo-Nazi group. In English it stands for Action and they pick a word in other languages. Greek is Aether the father of the earth the sea and the heavens. Could be trouble. T.*

Tariq had this way of stating the blindingly bloody obvious as though his undoubted technical wizardry was the only early-warning system in existence. The big man on the roof looked dangerously like the tip of an unseen army of soldiers.

Suzi read it. 'Let's get some lunch,' she said. 'Need some fuel.'

I protested, but she was right on three things: we couldn't stop being tourists; running around like headless chickens wasn't going to get us anywhere; without food we'd be useless in a few hours. Biologically, we're a sack of water that learned to walk on land.

We ate a seafood platter with, by unspoken agreement, a bottle of ginger beer because we needed to stay sharp. Then another swimming lesson. She was off and away with the breast stroke, her golden hair bobbing above the water. The problem was, the better she got the less I could hold her. We splashed about like a couple of kids without a care in the world, but we knew in our hearts that we were getting into waters far darker and more dangerous than these shallows.

*

I grabbed a couple of hours' kip, freshened-up, and went out to eat around eight. There was an Italian place just up the harbour road before *Nafsika* and I decided that might be worth a try, because I'd seen the wood-burning oven, and I'd actually eaten fish that day – how's that for a good boy, Maria? – and a pizza sounded like a brilliant idea. I munched my way through a *quattro stagioni* while I read my book, trying to relax but I was really tense. Two images kept coming to mind: Tina with her open smile, and Tina cold and suspicious in her office. And you can add to that a man who could well be a killer standing on the roof of an abandoned hotel.

It squanders a book when you're reading with other things on your mind. Somehow your eyes still scan the pages but you're not *in* it.

At ten o'clock I paid up and left. I walked back into the village. *Zorba*'s was full of people eating under the big parasols. *Bar38* had plenty of customers. *Condor* had a karaoke night and was packed, the music loud but lively.

I carried up the incline until I came the *Silver Moon* and turned down the side road towards the mysterious building, although I had no intention of getting too close. I was wearing dark clothes and kept to the shadows from the apartment block's pool and bar lights. There was no sign of life that I could detect and I doubted there was an electric supply turned on in a building in that state of disrepair. In which case, what was the big man doing there?

On my way back down the main drag I was passing *Condor* when I saw Tina and Suzi get up from a side table and march to the front. They were wearing short dresses – all legs. Then it started: they grabbed the mikes, told the DJ what they wanted, and off they went. They were Beyoncé and Shakira doing *Beautiful Liar*. I was prepared to wince, but, fuck me, they were terrific. Had they been rehearsing? The singing was spot on and they danced there with hips swinging, turning and spinning like a couple of pros. Golden and brown hair – blonde and brunette – swirling across their eyes.

I thought I'd seen it all, but I was hypnotised.

And a bit peeved that they weren't consciously doing it for me. They ended with a huge round of applause and calls for more. The thing is they looked really happy together – two beautiful liars strutting their stuff on a balmy Greek night.

Bang. They were off again with *Lady Marmalade*, swapping vocal parts, harmonising, thrusting their pelvises backwards and forwards and pouting as they sang *Volulez-vous couchez avec moi ce soir?* They were a living wet-dream. I'd already got my phone on video record. There was quite a crowd around me on the pavement watching this and clapping along. I had a terrible urge to go in and dance but I was also feeling obscurely left out and sulky, because being "under-cover" did not usually mean giving a stonking public performance of a rock anthem with a prime suspect.

They bowed and sat down with three other women and I could see the barman bringing a couple of complimentary drinks over and ceremoniously delivering them. I had a new understanding of what a girlie night out was like. A lot better than going out on the piss with the lads.

The crowd melted away down the street and I went with them. Back in my room I plugged my headphones in and watched them again. Six times.

CHAPTER EIGHTEEN

I bought croissants and custard-tart like things in the bakery, and butter and jam in the supermarket next door. To be honest, the Greeks can't really do croissants; maybe it's the flour but they are a bit too chewy, but hell, who's complaining? The village was buzzing with bikes and vans. You only see men at this time in the morning, carrying bags of bread like prizes of the hunt to their women, who were probably still yawning in their nighties.

When I got back to *Artemis* they were both behind the bar – Tina making coffee and Suzi scrubbing the bar down with a cloth as though she worked there. They saw me coming up the path and shared some secret joke, no doubt at my expense, because if you get women together in groups of more than one and they don't actively hate each other they will close ranks in an instant. I was outgunned. Suzi, I had to admit, was doing a bloody good job. She'd got Tina's confidence, she'd got as far as the bar, and before long she'd get access to the office.

I held the bag up and said 'Morning ladies. Breakfast. Good night out?'

'Just a quiet one,' said Tina as she loaded the coffee machine. My mobile is not the latest all-singing all-dancing ludicrously expensive slice of silicon you could get, but it's plenty loud. I held it up and those lounging about by the pool turned their heads as the thumping beat of *Lady Marmalade* rang out.

'If that's quiet,' I said as I turned it down a bit, 'I'd hate to think what loud is like.'

They laughed and Tina said 'Been snooping, have you, Johnny?'

'Snooping? Not much need to snoop with about a hundred decibels or whatever drawing a crowd in the street. Can I be your manager? North Corfu tour. I bet half the men in the village came into their boxers.'

Tina pushed a mug of tea across the counter. 'Including you?' she asked with a sweet smile.

'I plead the Fifth. Anyway, I'm glad you had a good time.'

Suzi said 'Best time I've had since I've been here. Really.' She got some small plates from behind the bar and we shared out the croissants and custard tarts. I tried to look suitably pissed-off, which wasn't that hard.

*

Later, sitting by the sea at *Havana*, Suzi brought me up to speed.

'I like her,' she said. 'I mean *really* like her. She's bright and funny. She can be quite dirty when she wants to be. We had dinner at *Zorba's* – Tina, me, the TUI rep, the Jet2 rep, and two women from *San Stefano Travel* – that's down by the beach.'

'I know where it is.'

'Don't interrupt. The thing is, while we were

eating Tina got a call on her mobile. She didn't look pleased – in fact, I'd say she was frightened. She went inside to the loos and came out fifteen minutes later. The mascara on her right eye was running a bit, as though she'd been crying. One of the reps asked her who it was, and she said it was an argument over a bill. I think it was more serious than that. Tina's tough – arguing over a bill would be second-nature to her. After a bit she calmed down and got into the flow.'

She paused and sipped her beer.

'Conclusions?' I asked.

'I think she might be being blackmailed.'

'Could be a love thing.'

'No. She'd have slagged him off and got a bit of female sympathy. This was definitely something else.'

'It's a bit thin,' I said 'You could be right or you could be wrong.'

'For fuck's sake, Johnny, you asked for a report and I'm giving you one.'

'Sorry. I bow to your superior knowledge of female psychology.'

'Don't be a patronising prick! I know it suits you but I've got a hangover and I can do without it today, thank you very much. Now order some lunch.'

I guess I couldn't grasp the difference between Suzi the DS who was my subordinate and the Suzi who was now notionally my equal. I was slipping back into being her DI and her calling me *Guv* and me deciding when we had lunch, but I knew she probably out-ranked me. I remembered the gun under the pillow. I wanted her to love me, but I was going about it entirely the wrong way. As usual. We sat and shared a club sandwich. I kept schtum and let it ride. She was a linguist and linguists need to talk, so I let her.

She finished her half of the sandwich before I'd coped with much of mine, and eventually she put her hand on my arm and said 'Sorry.'

I smiled at her and said nothing.

'There are a couple of other things,' she said. 'She has a private pilot's license.'

'So, she'd be pretty good at flying drones.'

'Yes. My thought exactly. She has a part share in a Cessna Skyhawk parked at the airport and she sometimes takes a few of the girls for a ride.'

'Just girls?'

'How the fuck would I know? Get real!'

'Just trying to establish the facts.'

'One night, Johnny. One fucking night and you expect miracles.'

'For what it's worth,' I said carefully 'I think you've done your usual fantastic job. You said there were two things.'

She sat back in her chair. Always a bad sign. 'God knows why, Johnny, but she really fancies you. And I have an idea.'

'What idea?' She shook her head and said 'Not yet. I need to think about it some more. One thing's for sure – we need to get her phone.'

'I agree. But all we really need is the number of whoever phoned her, and that's not likely to help much if it's a burner.'

'Johnny – Tina inherited a lot of money. She's rich. She does not need to take part in smuggling to make a few quid. Why would she? She's defo not stupid. I don't get the impression that she's a right-wing fanatic, so I doubt if she would help the neo-Nazis willingly. It's all pointing to blackmail.'

She was right. 'I really hope you're right about this, and just this once I agree with you. Get closer to her.'

'I can't try any harder without looking clingy.'

'Fair enough. Trouble is, I have to go home in five days, and I have to report to Maria.'

'See if the room's still free and extend it. If not, I've got a spare room.'

'I think I need to have a face to face with Maria. Soon.'

She thought about it. 'The phone might be better. She knows something and I need you on the ground here.'

At which point my mobile started ringing. Sophia. 'You and Suzanne same place in Sidari as soon as possible.' She cancelled the call, and I told Suzi what she said.

'Who the fuck is she, Suzi?'

'Maybe *she'll* tell you. Let's go.'

Suzi driving in a hurry is not something you want to experience. All right, she was bloody good at it, but that didn't help even if you knew she knew the maximum cornering speed she could get away with in the souped-up Suzuki. I swear we coated the road to Sidari with rubber and had every bus driver in the region kissing the icons they had dangling from their wing-mirrors. I should have censored the "as soon as possible" into something like "in a reasonable time" but it was too late. I tightened my seat-belt and gripped the edges of my seat like a nervous grandma in a fun-fair and felt utterly bloody helpless.

I swear she did over a hundred-and twenty down the Avliotes bypass.

'Do you really want to draw all this attention?' I asked, more in hope than expectation, over the whine of the engine as she took the roundabout at the end in a death-defying assault on physics. In *Sidari* she turned left by *The Three Little Pigs* in a way that must have had the drivers of the garbage van and the hire car she slotted in between shitting themselves. I had an uncomfortable feeling I was.

My legs were trembling as we made the short walk up from the beach car park to the café. She was wearing the smug smile that always wound me up. Not for the first time I felt like I should have done my English degree and had a quiet life attempting to get a load of bored fifteen-year-olds to like Shakespeare. I had just been the victim in an exercise entirely designed to humiliate me. I was out-classed and I knew it. Is there a feminine equivalent to the noun *machismo*? I was surrounded by it – Maria, Tina, Suzi, Sophia.

We were sitting in the café sipping iced coffee when Sofia came in. She spoke to the owner and came over to us.

'That was quick,' she said.

'Too bloody quick. Hi Sophia.'

She sat down and looked sternly at Suzi. 'You have that car for emergencies, not to play at being a formula one driver. This is not an emergency. When it is, I can protect you. You drive fast but not stupid fast. Is clear?'

Suzi looked a bit downcast. 'Sorry,' she said. 'I need to know how to handle it at high speed.'

I was enjoying this. Maybe I wasn't such a wimp after all. Maybe I'm not a wimp – maybe I'm logical and sensible and assess the situation. Maybe I'm talking bollocks.

'We're not here to discuss this,' Sophia said. 'But I don't want you to get stopped by the police. Now behave. Enough!'

The café owner put a Greek coffee and a glass of water down for Sophia. Suzi was suitably subdued, and I'd decided to shut up and listen just for once. Although something was bugging me.

'Sophia,' I asked. 'Are you permitted to tell me exactly who you are?'

'No. But I will. Let's just say European counter-terrorism. That's enough for now.'

'We're not in Europe any more. So why are we involved?'

'You didn't sail your little island out to the Bahamas, Johnny. Europe is a continent and you're still part of it. Now please be quiet and listen.'

I made placatory gestures. Sophia made sure there was enough distance between us and anybody else before she continued.

'I need you to know this. Our intelligence tells us that Russia is supporting a movement designed to destabilise the entire Balkan region. We don't know all the details. We do know that Corfu has a part in it. Your work is helping. Everything you find out helps.' She paused and took a sip of her coffee. 'I have tried to get more resources here. I control the north of the island. But there is a limit and Athens thinks there are more important places. Like Athens, of course. I do not have enough people. I cannot get more people. How can I say – you are on your own?'

There was a long silence until I said 'Timescale?'

Suzi and Sophia talked for a moment in Greek, and Suzi said 'Maybe two to three weeks.'

'But I only have a few days,' I said.

Sophia smiled. '*Artemis* will have a cancellation in the morning. Deal with it.'

She got up and was about to go, then stopped. 'Listen,' she said. 'This is dangerous. You must be very careful. I cannot get replacements. There is a delivery at Suzanne's house.'

She walked out.

CHAPTER NINETEEN

Suzi drove at a reasonable speed on the way back. I made no comment. It's fair to say I'm an averagely incompetent male, but I know when to keep my bloody mouth shut. As we started our descent into the village I just ventured 'Why do some people call it *Agios Stefanos* and other people call it *San Stefanos*?'

'I don't know if it's true or not, but the story goes like this: there are two villages called *Agios Stefanos* on north Corfu, one in the east and this one in the west. This one has a long sandy beach. The other one has pebbles. Yuppies prefer the pebbles because girls who think they're posh don't like getting sand in their itsy-bitsy bikinis, or their bits for that matter.

'Thomson used to do packages to both villages, but the reps at the airport often put people on the wrong bus. The people who wanted to go to the pebbly bit were upset to find sand and working-class people in this village, and the people who wanted to come here were pissed-off when they saw nothing but pebbles and espadrilles.

'Faced with a serious problem, Thomson decided to rename this village in Spanish since working-class people obviously don't know the difference between Greek and Spanish and probably don't give a stuff. It's a bit of a bone of contention here because some of the locals think the real name of the village is being despised and others think it's good marketing – like a brand. People who come here a lot call it Ag Stef or San Stef or both.'

I was pleased that we were diverting ourselves away from dangerous topics. So was she.

'Where do you stand – or rather sit – on the issue of sand in the knickers?'

'Mind your own bloody business!'

When she parked at the top of the rise near to her little villa there was an anonymous white van there, and when we walked past the shrine and reached the bungalow there were two big men and a wooden crate. They didn't speak. They compared us with photos on their phones, waited for Suzi to open up, and carried the crate inside. Suzi told them to put the crate in the spare bedroom, and they left as soon as they'd done it, without saying a word.

I tried to lift one side of the crate with my left hand; it was very heavy, maybe steel-lined.

'What is it?' I asked.

'I have a horrible suspicion that Sophia wasn't kidding.' She knelt down beside the crate with her mobile phone and waited. After a few seconds a blue rectangle appeared on her phone. She pressed her thumb on it. There was a click from the crate. The lid was easy to remove, revealing a plastic foam rectangle, which she lifted off. The interior had shaped foam anti-shock compartments keeping the contents safe from shock.

'Fucking hell!' was all I could say. A satellite phone, two Heckler & Koch VP70 military grade semi-automatic hand guns, spare cartridges and stacks of ammunition, amongst other things. 'Where's the rest of NATO?'

There was small piece of paper. She looked at it and handed it to me.

'Our idents,' she said. 'Bonnie and Bandit.'

We replaced the lid and Suzi thumbed her phone again. The lid locked. 'It'll open for you as well,' she said. 'At least I think it will.'

I tried. It did.

We went outside and burned the paper in the barbecue, crushing the ashes and spreading them around the stubby-grassed garden.

*

San Stefano Travel is a low and unusual building with blue woodwork. It has two doors: one on the harbour road corner and other on the way to the beach. It was evening when we went in past the colourful pictures of sea-trips and coach tours. Inside there were three areas with desks, the first one empty. The two women at the other desks, one Greek and one English, were friendly and helpful when we booked a small boat for the next day. It turned out we could go quite a long way if we wanted to – north-east to *Sidari* or south-west to *Paleokastritsa*. That wasn't on our agenda, but we didn't say so.

We had supper in *Manthos,* and very nice it was

looking out over the sea with the pink after-glow of the sunset, and planned for tomorrow. That's when Suzi dropped her bomb-shell.

'You're the expert at tactics,' she said. 'What's our next move?'

'What I don't get is what's so important about this place,' I said. 'It's designed for holidays. Full stop. There are no soldiers, the airport's miles away across the mountains, it's not a naval base. I don't see any strategic value at all. Not a thing.'

'There has to be something.'

'So why hasn't Sophia told us?'

'I don't think they know. Intelligence work is putting together lots of small hints until you get a picture.'

'Like police work. We're just the ones sorting the grist from the chaff or whatever in this corner of the jigsaw.'

'So, who knows what's going down?'

'Certainly the man I saw at the abandoned building. Possibly Tina.'

'Can we try to get him? We could arrive tooled up with the H&Ks and see what he has to say when he's face-down with two muzzles pointing at him.'

'Not a good idea. Yet. We'd blow our cover and there could be half a dozen of them for all we know. Far too risky.'

'I agree. Do you think Tina's attractive?'

I shrugged. 'She's all right.'

'Under different circumstances, if you got a chance to get into her probably rather expensive

panties, would you pretend you'd taken a vow of
celibacy and just have another beer?'

'Are you suggesting what I think you're suggesting?'

'I'm suggesting our holiday fling ends abruptly
at the right moment and you seek solace.'

It simply hadn't crossed my mind. Well – that's
not entirely true, to be honest. Of course it had. I'd
spent enough time with pathologists to know that
beneath the calm logical control of the cortex in
the brain lies the limbic system, the bit of us that
is part jelly-fish, part crocodile, part ape. Try as we
may to control it the bugger will do its own thing –
and Tina hit all the right buttons to get the primitive juices flowing. Until, that is, Suzi turned up.
Suzi did it all for me.

And now she was asking me to forget her and
sleep with Tina.

'Out of the question,' I said.

'It's never out of the question. There are times
when we have to do these things to get under
the barbed wire. It's the only way I can think of
to break Tina down, and if we don't then Christ
knows what shit is going to happen in our patch.
If you could have stopped nine-eleven or seven-
seven or the Manchester arena attack by getting
your dick out would you have said *no*?'

*

Suzi picked me up at eight in the morning and
we drove to the harbour. Our little white boat was
ready - fuelled-up, with a sunshade over the top

and fat outboard on the back; no tiller, but a steering wheel and electric start. Suzi paid, so it wasn't on my budget. I took the big cool-bag out of the car and put it on the quay beside the boat and Suzi reached up from the boat and stowed it in the shade. Suzi started the engine, and I cast off before climbing in. We put our life-jackets on and I said 'Remember – the phrase is *pottering* about, not trying to break the sound barrier.'

'Aye aye Captain. Steering north north-east out of the harbour, Captain sir.'

The huge rocks of the harbour boom slipped by and soon we were out on the sea. We turned to the south-west around the tip of the headland and across the bay in front of the next village, *Arillas*, towards another promontory, where the windows of houses flashed in the morning light high over the Ionian waters.

'Permission to increase speed slightly, Captain?'

'Fuck off Suzi. Just be sensible.'

'I bet Horatio Nelson wasn't this boring.'

'He had a glamorous mistress. I guess it helps.'

'So could you soon. Think about it. Captain.'

I decided to shut up and not give her the pleasure. The sun was warm but still too low to be above the shade over the boat. Suzi stripped off her shorts and top and steered the boat standing up in her bikini. It was impossible not to notice the smooth roundness of her bum under the tight yellow fabric. We were probably supposed to find some secluded beach where we could roll naked in the surf and do stuff. If that was what she fancied I certainly wasn't going to argue, but I sure as hell didn't want to risk a kick in the balls by suggesting it. I consulted the pretty map we'd be given, stood up beside her and put my left arm gently around her.

'Left around that point and slow down into *Porto Timon*i,' I said. She saluted.

We chugged our way sedately in towards a beautiful beach which had a spit of land separating it from another beach. A few people were scrambling down a cliff-path. Suzi killed the engine and there was just the sound of little waves lapping against the boat and the cries of a few sea-birds.

I sighed. 'Why is life such shit?' I said.

She smiled. 'It's only shit when you realise how *not* shit it could be.'

There was a thermos flask of iced coffee in the cool-bag and we stretched out on the seats and sipped it from cold mugs. The boat moved gently in the imperceptible swell. A few gulls swooped low over us hoping we'd have some fish for them. Lazy bastards, gulls – nasty loud opportunists and thieves.

Inevitably, Suzi had to break the moment. 'Have you thought about what I said last night?'

'Of course I've bloody thought about it. A lot. It's not practical.'

'Explain.'

'It'll take too long even if it works, which I doubt. What would somebody as sophisticated and well-off as Tina want with a damaged ex-cop?'

She did a very good impression of Michelle in *'all 'allo.* 'Listen very carefully. I will say zis only once. You are borderline very handsome. You are clever and funny and intelligent. You are wounded but strong. And she fancies your god-forsaken arse. Get real.'

Fuck me rigid. I never thought I'd hear her say something like that. That was outside the rules of our usual *I put you down, you put me down* game. There was a long silence. When she spoke it was quiet and far away from the usual banter.

'Johnny... I know you have – feelings – for me. I've known for a long time. There is only one man I would ever have wanted to be in this with me, and it's you, you dumb fuck. When you held me in the darkness the nightmares went away and I felt safe. Safe with you. If you'd made love to me then I might actually have been happy. You didn't, even though you wanted to. I could feel you against me. I wanted you like I've never ever wanted that before. I nearly put my hand down there. But I didn't and you didn't touch me.'

She took a pause for breath. 'This is not what I want. This is a million miles from what I want, Johnny. But it's all we've got. Stop being a gentleman.'

She hit the starter button and the engine roared into life. 'Back to work,' she said. The boat turned back out to sea and she gunned the engine. The prow lifted and a V-shaped white wake trailed us, foaming the deep blue water. She steered us out to-wards the nearest island with just one hopeful gull soaring above us.

'This is *Diaplo*,' Suzi said. 'It's split down the middle.' Indeed it was – an island cleaved in two by titanic forces lost in the mists of time. We roared through the gap with the sound of the engines echoing off the low cliffs on each side. When we were through she swung the boat around and we slowed until we were on the opposite side from the shore. The sea was breaking on the rocks not so far from us when she stopped the engine.

I unzipped the cool-bag and took out the H&K machine pistol. A loaded magazine was wrapped in a plastic bag, and I took it out and clipped it into the gun. The safety was on. I checked twice. We could not fire it anywhere near the village – not even up in the olive groves – but here we were shel-tered from the village and the sound would not carry. Suzi pointed out a rock spire on the shore. I nodded.

Only an idiot would fire an automatic in burst mode with one hand. I'm right-handed but there was no way I was going to use this dangerous thing in my damaged hand. We'd discussed it. Instead I gripped the gun in my left hand and crooked my right arm into a rest, nestling the gun inside my elbow. It wasn't ideal. My firearms training ser-geant would have shat himself.

'Single shot,' she said.

'Check.'

'Go for it.'

I aimed and pulled the trigger. Loud crack, and dust flew up to the left and up from the rock. Bummer. Guns kick upwards. I aimed and fired two more rounds, with direct hits on the rock.

'Try burst,' she said. I did. It was violent, loud and made my hand ache like hell. A hail of bullets traced a line of flying debris down the face of the rock.

'Acceptable,' she said as she kicked the engine back into life. 'You'll do.'

We went at a moderate pace back past the twin-beach headland point of *Porto Timoni* and the village of *Afionas* above it and crossed the wide sweep of *St George's Bay*. I only knew this because I had the map. Looking in towards the land we could see a long sandy beach with hotels and tavernas tiny in the distance. A couple of seagulls took station above us – plainly not from the bunch which had crapped themselves when I fired the machine pistol and who were now probably somewhere over Turkey still screaming alarm cries.

The lovely women at *San Stefano Travel* had provided helpful information about good spots to eat on our boat trip and put some crosses on the map for us. More likely, for me. The Ms Overachiever I was with could probably memorise the entire Michelin Guide in thirty seconds. Way out in the bay on the far side there was a fish taverna with a good reputation called *The Fisherman's Cabin*. We parked (is that the word?) at the little jetty and ate fresh sardines with a Greek salad, bread, and a bottle of dry white wine. For once, Suzi ate slowly. When I asked why, she said she was nervous of fish bones and liked to have plenty of bread in her mouth when she ate small fish. I smiled. It's the little things - know what I mean?

We didn't talk much, and when we did we managed to stay off the subject of work. Our phones were mercifully silent. After I poured the last of the wine into our glasses she took my right hand very gently and kissed it, her eyes focused on mine. She still held it gently as the taverna owner brought a plate of sliced cold water-melon and some little glasses of *Raki*.

We sailed up the southern side of the bay and around the headland, where the cliffs grew ever taller, and then into a little inlet – totally deserted – a tiny sandy beach with sheer planes of rock on either side. Suzi ran the boat up onto the beach and we climbed off and pulled it further up the sand until it was secure. The sun was hot as she sank into the water and lay floating on her back for a few seconds and then came to me, put her arms around me and kissed me on the mouth. I mean, really kissed me, her eyes closed as our mouths opened and our tongues met. She reached behind her back and her bikini top fell onto the beach. Her nipples were firm and sea-wet against my chest. I reached down and her bikini bottom slid away at the same time as she stripped my swimming shorts off. We lay on the edge of lapping water and kissed long kisses until we touched each other and her legs twined around my back and we came together in wonderful convulsions of love and pleasure.

Then we made love again, standing, she leaning back against the boat with her arms spread along the side, whispering erotic suggestions into my ear. When the trembling died down we went into the sea to cool off, towelled down and put our clothes on.

Suzi being Suzi she had to say something to put me in my place. She waited until the boat was heading back to the harbour, turned to me and said 'Very satisfactory trip. All equipment appears to be in working order.'

If I'd thought I had the slightest chance of success I'd have chucked her over the side.

CHAPTER TWENTY

I sat at the *Artemis* pool bar counter on a stool looking a bit downcast. Tina had noticeable dark rings under her eyes, so neither of us were exactly the heralds of a bright seaside day. Truth to tell I was feeling down. Suzi both amazed me and pissed me off. I could totally see the logic of her idea, but at the same time I hated it. The reality of making love with her had been as fantastic as I'd hoped for a long time that it would be. I'd gone over it time after time in my mind, hoping that I wasn't just a convenient pawn in the Intelligence game and meant something to her. But if I refused to go along with the plan I would have let her down. Or would I? What did she want? Did she want me to refuse as a declaration of love or would it make me forever a loser? Had she screwed one or many as part of her job? Did she care? Had she been trained in faking sexual pleasure at some MI6 school for good-looking operatives?

Tina put a mug of tea, some sugar and an ashtray in front of me, and then pushed a saucer with some Hobnobs on it across as well.

'Heavy night?' she asked.

I shook my head. 'Not really. Not at all.'

'Oh. I thought you were having a good time.'

I sighed. 'I was. Just one of those things. Look – I'm due to fly back on Tuesday. I don't feel like it.

Do you have a spare room?'

'You can have your room for another couple of weeks, if you like. It's early in the season and I can juggle things a bit.'

'You are a star. How much?'

'Tell you what. If you help out with this bar now and then you can have it at half-price.'

I cheered up. 'That is amazing,' I said. 'Of course. I'll change my flight.'

Last night I'd been listening from a distance as Suzi had a heart-to-heart with Tina on the phone. She was engaged to a barrister in Leeds and was feeling guilty and a bit worried that I was getting all clingy and hopeful. She was probably telling the truth about the last part.

'Suzi having second thoughts?' Tina asked.

'You could put it like that.'

'What happened.'

'Well – something on her phone upset her. Then I put my foot in it.'

She sipped her coffee. After a pause she said 'And?'

'She asked me to read a bit of her novel. I was not adequately enthusiastic, it seems.'

'She probably wanted some encouragement. That's normal. I had a writer staying here last year – scrawny old man – bit full of himself – always right. You know the sort? His partner read what he'd been writing and said it was no good, so he ripped it up and set light to it. I must say I felt a bit sorry for him – he'd been sitting by the pool

cheerfully writing for a couple of hours a day. But –
there you go – sensitive souls and all that. Come on.
You're supposed to be on holiday.'

The fact is, I'd read some of the fake novel and it
was a complete load of old toss. But I'd seen some
of Suzi's and it showed promise of actually being
good. I didn't tell her that because she was too
bloody cocky by half as it was. That's how we came
up with an additional reason for us falling out. I
put on a brave smile. 'I'd better organise a flight,'
I said. And went upstairs. I was pretty sure Tina
would phone Suzi in the meantime.

I came back down with a beach-bag packed, but
Tina called me over.

'Fancy a ride?' she asked. 'See a bit of the island.
Might take your mind off it.'

'Are you sure?'

'Would I ask you if I wasn't? Go and put some
trousers on and bring your passport.'

*

There was a small queue of passengers outside
Departures at the airport, with *Jet2* reps in their
bright red uniforms passing up and down issuing
instructions, a bit like shepherds herding sheep.
Tina led the way inside to the Olympic office,
where she paid some money on her cards and filled
in forms. She seemed to be having a lot of cheerful
banter with the reps in Greek. They looked at me
curiously and one said something that sounded
suspiciously like "mile high club" and "autopilot."
Tina laughed and said 'Five thousand feet.' I

checked on my phone and five thousand feet is point nine four miles.

'Make it six thousand,' I said, and she dug me in the ribs with her elbow.

Paperwork stamped and initialled and we went to another office and did it all over again. Tina sighed and turned to me.

'Greek bureaucracy is alive and well. This is one of the few airports in the world where you can't walk to the General Aviation area. So now we have to wait for a bus or a van. Take a seat.' Half an hour later a radio crackled in the room, the official pointed at the door, and we went through the security checkpoint. We had the long bus to ourselves for the one-minute ride up the apron to where private planes were parked. There weren't many planes there, just two corporate jets and a small white plane with a propeller. Tina handed the driver a ten-euro tip as we walked off the bus.

'Be thankful we always take on fuel when we get back,' she said. 'You can wait an hour if it's busy because they have to go back and swap from jet fuel to avgas. Planes are fast – airports are slow.'

She opened the door of the Cessna and stowed her bag. 'Now I have to inspect the plane,' she said, and I walked around with her as she checked everything – propeller, tyres, body-work, hatches, various tubes and obscure things sticking out of the side. Finally satisfied, she climbed into the left-hand seat and I went around and climbed into the one on the right. She showed me how to put the harness on and passed me an A4 sheet of paper heat-sealed in plastic with the words "Pre-start checklist" in bold print at the top. She put her headset on and told me to do the same. When she flicked a switch the instruments on the dashboard – if that's the right word – came to life and I could suddenly hear her in in my headphones. I read down the list, item by item as she adjusted things and checked things, none of which made any sense to me.

'This is important, Johnny,' she said. 'If I tell you to do something you do it immediately, no questions. Got it?' Of course I got it. I am not James Bond. I could no more fly this thing than I could land on the moon.

She pulled the stick with half a steering wheel on it forward and back and side to side, then spoke to Air Traffic Control on the radio.

'Cessna Oscar Lima Bravo niner seven request engine start. Cessna niner seven.'

The reply was instant: 'Tower . Cessna niner seven Kalimera start engine, taxi and hold short taxiway alpha.'

'Start engines and hold short alpha – Cessna niner seven'

It was bloody loud when the engine started. The propeller flicked a couple of times and then roared into life. Needles waggled on dials and she waited until the engine warmed up before releasing the parking brake. We moved slowly forward until we reached a red line just before the end of the runway, where she stopped. I could see why – a big jet came rapidly down over the hill to our right and came in to land. As it passed I could see the blue fuselage, and the yellow *Tui* smile on the tail gleamed for a moment before it was out of sight down the runway.

Then we waited some more as a *Condor* jet taxied out onto the runway near us and accelerated away into the distance.

'Can't we go now?' I asked.

'We have to wait. That Airbus is leaving nasty twisting wind behind it that could flip us over.'

Thanks a lot. I was sitting in a small plane with a woman who was probably complicit in some ghastly crime in a situation totally out of my control and I did not want to hear about twisty winds and planes flipping over with me inside.

The tower cleared us for take-off. We eased forward until we were looking straight down the runway. Tina spun the engine up, and the terminal was on our left as we accelerated towards the sea and the sky to the south. It wasn't long before we lifted off with plenty of tarmac still in front of us. Tina talked to Air Traffic Control as we climbed out over a long concrete boom and a little white church on an island. It wasn't like being in a passenger jet – more like being a fast car.

Tina banked the plane to the left and we came around until we were flying to the north with the runway and terminal to our left and once we'd passed the hill beside the airport, Corfu Town lay below us, with harbours and sea on the right.

'See the castles – two of them? That's the Old Fort and the New Fort. They helped keep the Ottomans out. We're proud of that. They never defeated us. We're the only part of Greece that never fell under Ottoman rule. Not bad for a small island, huh?'

'Very impressive. Didn't work against the Germans or the British, though.'

'The Germans brought us pain. The British brought us cricket. The Ottomans didn't have much to offer. To be honest, by the time we're talking about, the Turkish empire was collapsing. Greece didn't exist as a country until eighteen twenty-two. Kerkyra wasn't much of a prize, really. But we don't mention that.'

We crossed a wide bay and flew up the coast. Albanian mountains stretched out on the right, and the passage between Corfu and Albania looked narrow. Tina pressed some knobs in front of her and took her hands off the control column. The dial in front of me showed five thousand feet. Ahead the island was a panorama of green slopes and a blue sea fringed with white and terracotta buildings. Boats left foamy trails.

'You're very lucky,' I said, 'being able to do this. Have to say, it's fantastic.'

'I need to fly to keep my licence. But you're right – it is fantastic. I feel free up here. It's the best time for me.'

I looked across at her and her face seemed more

relaxed than I'd seen it. The radio chattered with voices between Air Traffic Control and various planes arriving or departing. Ahead, the land to our left grew steeper and more mountain than hill until we were heading towards a high peak.

'What's that?'

'That is Mount Pantokrator – the highest point of the island.'

'Do we go round it?'

'No. Over it. It's just under three thousand feet. Plenty of room.'

I checked the dial in front of me. We were flying steadily at five thousand feet.

'What if the engine fails?'

'See that blue stuff on the right? If we can't glide back to the airport we land on the sea. There's nowhere to land near here. There's a life-jacket under your seat. Don't you trust me?'

'I don't have much choice, do I?'

She thumbed a switch on the dashboard and transmitted. 'Request climb to six thousand feet Cessna niner seven.'

'Cessna niner seven, climb and maintain six thousand.'

'Climb and maintain six thousand Cessna niner seven.'

She turned a knob on the panel in front to six thousand and pressed the knob. The nose lifted and the needle on the dial in front of me started winding clockwise. She was smiling.

'Well you did ask for six thousand,' she said.

There were buildings on top of the mountain. A tall spire of steel rose from inside some walls. I could see a café with a few cars parked beside it and a lot of smaller masts in an enclosure nearby.

'That mast was built inside a monastery in the time of the Colonels to provide TV for the island. The Church objected. The Colonels told the monks to go and play with themselves and built it anyway. That's how it was in those days.'

'What's all that other stuff?'

'Mobile phone masts.'

'Got you.'

We passed over the mountain and ATC told us to go down to four thousand feet. In front of us there was a big village or town with a harbour. Tina pointed out the sights. 'That's *Kassiopi* – the biggest village on the island. Venetian port.'

She banked the plane to the left and we flew along the northern coast as she reeled off the names of the villages and resorts. I forgot the mission and everything else. This was beautiful, watching the beaches roll by below us. At *Sidari* we turned left again and flew over *Agios Stefanos*. She nosed the plane down a bit and flew low over *Artemis* and then away over *Arillas* and headed back cross-country to the airport. She switched off the autopilot and took control as we circled, waiting for permission to land. We went down steeply and sunk onto the runway, carrying on to a turning circle at the south, then back up the runaway and our parking spot. She called the tower, ordered fuel, and shut the engine down. The silence was startling – I'd forgotten how loud it had been.

Tina sat in the cockpit filling in her log book. After a while a truck arrived towing a fuel bowser and a bus arrived for us.

'Let me give you some petrol money,' I said. She shook her head.

'Next time. Next time you can fly it.'

'You've got to be kidding.'

'Planes like to fly. That's what they do. If they're properly trimmed they'll fly themselves quite happily. It's the same for airliners and this Cessna. Military fighters are different – they're unstable and they need constant adjustments. You can't fly them without computers.'

'What about my hand?'

'You'll be fine. Trust me.'

She paid her fuel bill with a platinum credit card, and we set off back on the winding hilly road to home. The thing is – I wanted to trust her but I couldn't. Flying a plane around like it was second nature was a demonstration of power of some sort. But I'd seen her relax up there, as though she'd left a load of trouble on the ground.

*

She dropped me off at *Artemis* and went home. There was a bag of groceries on the table. I turned on the laptop and opened a secure link to Suzi. She sounded peeved.

'Had a nice time flying around with Captain Gorgeous?' she said.

'Yes, thank you.'

'Good. While you were out I came over and dropped some things. The maid – Zoe – was running the bar. I told her I needed to put milk and yoghurt in your fridge. She gave me the master key. I went into room twelve and swabbed the bag.'

'Brilliant.'

'Wasn't it just? I've just got some results back from the analyser.'

'And?'

'It's not heroin. It's Semtex or C-4. This is not smuggling – it's terrorism.'

'My fucking Aunt Ada!'

'You need to stop talking like that. She won't like it. If we don't find out what she's doing and who she's doing it with within forty-eight hours I'll have to get her picked up and interrogated. You need to up your game ASAP.'

'Listen Suzi – she was really happy flying the plane. It was like she was another person. I think she's under pressure.'

'You really are a sucker, Johnny. I think she's a calculating bitch who wouldn't mind a quick screw especially if it got one over me. Find the bloody weak spot. Fast!'

She closed the connection. Maybe Arsenal versus Chelsea tonight would take my mind off it.

CHAPTER TWENTY-ONE

At half-past six my phone rang. It was Tina.

'What are you doing tonight?'

'I'm going to watch Arsenal thrash Chelsea and have moussaka in *Little Prince*.'

'You can't watch football on your own. I've got Sky and I've made *pastitsio*.'

'Remind me. What's that?'

'Local dish. Minced beef and macaroni with cinnamon and red wine baked in a cheese sauce. Fancy that?'

'Do I ever! But how do I get to you?'

'Taxi will pick you up at eight o'clock. Don't bring anything.'

'Can I wear my Arsenal shirt? I've got you down for a Chelsea fan.'

'Course you can. Wait and see.'

It was a big house – much bigger than I expected – standing back behind high walls and ornate wrought-iron gates which opened when the taxi pulled up. I'd taken a diversion to Nafsika on the way and Spiros had sold me a bottle of a red wine called *Limniona*, which he assured me was excellent. It wasn't cheap. The taxi driver laughed when he saw it and made a gesture with his fist that didn't need translating.

Tina opened the door and stood to one side. She was wearing a knee-length black skirt and an Arsenal shirt – an Arsenal *women's* shirt. I laughed.

'Very good!'

'I prefer to dress for the top team.' We high-fived and I handed her the bottle of vino. 'I told you not to bring anything. Naughty boy. Nice, though.'

'How do you say "wine" in Greek?'

'*Krasí*. Kra-SEE. Come on through.'

White walls, blue woodwork, glass doors looking out over a terrace with a swimming pool. Expensive-looking furniture, a dining table, and a long sofa facing about eighteen-hundred quid's-worth of LG sixty-five-inch TV with another grand's worth of Bose soundbar in front of it. Jesus – and a PlayStation Five and a top-range sound system and CD player. There was a glossy magazine called "Holles Connect" on the coffee table by the sofa – looked like a trap for wealthy old alumni of her school. She probably sponsored flying lessons for the girls.

'Wow, Tina.' I said. 'This is fabulous.'

'Thank you. It suits me.'

'I should bloody hope so!'

'When you live on your own you need a bit of entertainment. The winters here are damp and cold. I just retreat in here, listen to music, watch football and play a few games. Fancy a gin and tonic?'

The kitchen was like an outpost of MasterChef happily free of John and Greg. You could have got half of my flat into the fridge. Ice rattled out of a spout on the front and into a glass bowl. She expertly sliced limes into pretty shapes and mixed some lethal-looking G&Ts.

The *pastitsio* was delicious, pasta tubes soft and the cheese sauce rich and fragrant.

'It doesn't seem very Greek,' I said.

'The food on Corfu is a kind of mixture of Greek and Italian. The island was once part of the Venetian empire and the influence remained. It was the Venetians who paid the islanders to plant all the olive trees and export olive oil and wine. Before that the Greeks owned large bits of southern Italy and Sicily. Empires come and go, but they leave their fingerprints in the food. Modern Greek cuisine is a mixture of Egyptian, Turkish, and what was here before.'

'Tina,' I said. 'Can I ask a rude question?'

'I'm sure you can. But, yes, you may.'

'How come you've got all this money?'

She wasn't fazed. Not in the slightest. She poised, fork in hand, and said 'My grandfather was basically a criminal. He owned lots of property in London and terrorised his tenants. He was violent and horrible and as close to pure evil as you can get. People got beaten up and thrown on the street. He had armed body-guards and a small army of sadistic enforcers. He made a lot of money. This is some of it, I'm afraid. I'm not proud of it.'

'You should be. This is a lovely house.'

'Sometimes I wish it wasn't. People suffered to give me this. I try not to think about it.'

'I'm sorry. I shouldn't have asked.'

'Of course you should! It's the truth about me.'

The music on the sound system changed from Mozart to jazz – cool Miles Davis at his peak as she took the plates away and brought a fruit salad.

'Kind of Blue,' I said.

'Greatest jazz record ever made.'

'So true.'

'What about you, Johnny? I don't ask guests in *Artemis* because that's their business, but – well – we're here.'

There wasn't much point lying about it. 'I was a copper. Not a very good one, it turned out. I thought I was but I wasn't.' I waved my dodgy hand. 'So, this and early retirement. Not very glamorous.'

'Will it recover? Fully?'

'Possibly. Possibly not.'

She raised her wine. 'Here's to it!' she said.

We clinked out glasses and finished the fruit, her deep brown eyes studying me across the table for a moment. Then we settled at opposite ends of the sofa and she told Alexa to turn the TV onto Sky Sports. The camera was high over the Emirates.

I imitated her well-spoken voice. 'Permission to bomb the Chelsea end. Cessna niner seven' I said, and she laughed. The camera focused on Mikel Artete's dark Spanish looks in the home team area behind the touchline

'Legend!' she shouted. It's a funny truth that a football match can totally change a supporter's personality. As the match progressed Tina got

195

louder and louder, jumping up off the sofa and shouting things like 'Fucking hopeless biased fucking referee! Piss off!' and 'How did you get a linesman's job, you blind twat! He was offside!'

Arsenal scored. We jumped into the air screaming 'Yes! Yes! Yes!'

Chelsea scored. We berated the officials for mistaking a clear foul for a legal tackle. We screamed at the VAR ref for siding with the officials. It was still one-all at half-time and Tina fetched a bottle of white wine and a bowl of Oregano crisps. 'It's much better when there's two of you,' she said in the quiet fifteen minutes that was like the still eye of an emotional hurricane. 'That's true for a lot of things,' I said, and she smiled. I was seeing a different Tina. She wasn't acting her passion for the Gooners – you can tell a real supporter from the millions who flocked to wear Man U's strip and abandoned them when they turned to shit. She was into it – big time.

Ten minutes in to the second half Lacazette smashed one past the Chelsea goalie and we leapt into the air side by side. We waited tensely for the VAR decision. Two-one to the Arsenal and we sank back onto the sofa and then leaned forward attentively as the ball pinged around the midfield. We challenged another Chelsea tackle but the ref wasn't listening.

Their defence was high up the pitch when Saka trapped a long cross-field pass and took off like a rocket. We rose to our feet. Chelsea were scrambling back but Saka was five yards ahead. One on one with the goalie. He jinked to the left, he jinked to the right, and slotted it perfectly into the net. We jumped together like a tribal dance.

One minute into time-added Saka did it again, this time after twisting around two defenders and shooting from an impossible angle near the goal line. The ball curved beyond the reach of the hapless blue shirts and into the top corner of the net. She screamed. I screamed. We hugged, arms around each other and danced up and down until the final triumphant whistle, laughing, charged with energy. We lay back, still entwined, and watched the match report, cheering Ian Wright as he said what a great performance the Arsenal had put on, sneering at John Terry as he tried to point out some lovely Chelsea moves.

When the credits rolled, Tina spoke to Alexa and the TV turned off as the stereo came on. Edith Piaf singing *Non, je ne regrette rien*. She climbed across and then astride me, her legs each side of mine, facing me. She leaned forwards and kissed me. Her tongue flicked out between the perfectly-whitened teeth and around my lips and then between them. She broke off the kiss only long enough to pull her red and white Arsenal ladies' strip over her head. Her breasts were not huge, but quite firm, dark disks of Mediterranean brown skin around her nipples. I ran my finger-nails down her spine. Her hair fell across my face.

I know what you're thinking. *What a bastard! No*

use pretending it was for the sake of the world. You were enjoying it. Look – I was compartmentalised. She was beautiful, she was fun, she was clever, she was wealthy, she was smart, she was an Arsenal supporter, and now she was completely animal. Maybe it was the football – I don't know. I don't think it was really me – I was an accessory to an urgent need. Did I enjoy it? Of course I bloody did.

We lay exhausted on her bed, her leg across my thighs, smiling. Her hand was on my stomach for a while and then she slid it down and cupped my balls in her fingers. And squeezed – gently at first and then harder until it started hurting. I winced. She squeezed harder.

'Why did Maria send you?' she whispered.

'Ease off and I'll tell you.' She didn't.

'I'm waiting,' she said.

I thought rapidly, in as much as it's possible to think when your testicles are in a vice-like grip with fingernails digging in. There was no point in pretending I didn't know what she was talking about. I said, through gritted teeth, 'She sent me to look after you.'

'To spy on me, you mean?'

'What are you afraid of, Tina? Maria's worried about you.'

She laughed. 'Maria hates me. Is that what she told you?'

'She was worried about something you were up to. Now let the fuck go of my bollocks and I'll talk. Really talk.'

The pressure eased off, but she kept her hand in place, and said 'Maria's not that bright. She's good at dishing out beta-blockers. If she was clever she'd have picked somebody who didn't have an office about a hundred yards away from her surgery. Nice website *John Almond Private Investigator.* So talk.'

'Okay. But I need you to talk, too.'

'We'll see. I think I'm holding all the spherical cards here.'

'Very few people know this. They really don't. Suzi and I were a team in the Serious Crime Squad. We got a message from an informer that a drug baron we were looking for had just holed up in a warehouse in Hackney. I decided this was too good a chance to pass up, and there was no time to bring in the heavy boys. I thought I could suss-out the place. I left Suzi hiding outside to cover the exit and went in. I wasn't good enough. I'd spent too much time sitting in my chair in the Stoke Newington nick doing bloody paperwork. Suzi told me not to, but I was her senior officer and she had to do what I said.

'He came at me from the side, fast. I dodged, but he hit me. Then I saw the machete as it swung toward me. He was on my right side so I put my right arm up to block him. If he'd have been stronger he'd have taken my hand off.

'The thing is, Tina. When I was a child they thought I was left-handed. I'm not. I am completely ambidextrous. He was off-balance. I got him by the throat with my left hand and I smashed him against the wall until he was dead. I didn't need to do that, but I wanted to. I smashed him again and again. We were covered with blood. So that's the truth, Tina. I'm a killer. So don't underestimate me.'

Her fingers let go and her hand moved up to stroke my face.

'That's terrible.'

'It was hushed up, and anyway it was pretty obvious I'd been attacked. What about you? What are you doing? Why are you doing it? I think I saw the real you today, up in the sky, and tonight. You were happy. Who's got to you?'

'You're a policeman.'

'Not anymore.'

'Same thing. Is a little bit of harmless smuggling such a crime?'

I picked up a lock of her hair and then let it drop gently onto her face.

'I'm here for you. I thought I was here for Maria – but now? I want to help. All I can.'

I felt her breath on my face. 'If I'd thought you and Suzi were an item – well- things would have been different.'

Were we? Now I wasn't sure.

'Identical twins are supposed to be very close, and we were. But. Maria always was more competitive than me. She just had to be captain of the Lacrosse team. She always said I lacked ambition. She hated anything less than straight "A" in exams. She really wants to do good as a doctor and help people – but not me, Johnny. She said I was the thick one. She said my MA in Business Studies was junk. That really hurt. I have made our side of the family very successful by dragging them kicking and screaming into the Twenty-first Century.

'I got my pathetic revenge. I slept with her husband, and made sure she found out. They got divorced. She seduced my lovely husband. It wasn't hard. We're identical. She knew all the buttons to press. He thought she was me with extras. I slung him out, but she'd had a word in a few ears and he was convicted of fraud and violent assault. He is not a violent man. See why I hate her?'

I tried to ignore my flaming crotch. The pain was spreading up to my stomach and down to my knees. She eased out of the bed, said 'Stay there a minute,' and went out of the bedroom. There was the sound of running water from the bathroom. For all I knew she could be using it to block the sound of her phoning somebody, or she could be getting a weapon. I eased my way off the mattress and limped over to the wall beside the door.

She came back, saw I wasn't in the bed and stopped in the doorway. 'Don't play silly-buggers, darling' she said. She held her hands out and I could see she was holding a wet flannel. We stood there, naked as Adam and Eve, and then she knelt down and gently pressed the cold flannel against my balls. After about thirty seconds the pain started to recede.

'What is it with you, Tina?' I asked. 'One minute you're a fucking KGB interrogator and the next you're Florence Nightingale.'

'Maybe I'm just a very confused person. Better?'

'Yes. It's getting better. How about some coffee?'

She took a couple of white towelling dressing gowns out of the walk-in wardrobe and we went through to the kitchen. The shiny Italian coffee machine hissed as she filled the filter-holder with freshly-ground dark beans.

'Four-one,' I said.

'If only we were at the Emirates!'

'Oh no – it was much better here in this beautiful house with you.'

'Don't get smarmy, Johnny. It doesn't suit you.'

'Smarmy or not – it *is* a beautiful house and you *are* a remarkable and beautiful woman. Me – I'm just a bloke who used to have testicles.'

She let the coffee drip into the china cups she'd set out and took some Amaretti biscuits out of a tin. Was this the moment? No point waiting.

'Smuggling what?'

'Oh, please don't go all DI Almond on me.'

'I'm serious. I don't give a flying toss whether Maria hates you or doesn't or whether Maria is worried about you or not. I'm worried about you. Very worried. Within a few hours, this place or wherever you are, will be surrounded by Greek police with some serious fire-power. I assume you have a gun here somewhere. They will press your dead fingers around it to get the prints to prove you shot first. You'll get maybe four through the heart and four headshots. Your brains and the back of your head will be all over a wall. There'll be some wavy dark hair stuck to it. The business empire you've built up will evaporate and nobody will deal with your family. The tour companies will pull out. Nobody will come for twenty years. The entire island will suffer. They won't bury your body here – they'll ship it back to the UK in a cardboard coffin to be cremated. Maria will hide her smile at your private funeral and drink a couple of Camparis.

'Tina – I am your only chance. Please take it. I don't want this to happen to you. And I promise you I am not bullshitting.'

I let her think about it as we sipped the hot coffee and nibbled the almond biscuits. Ironic, that. We were eating my name. Then the tears started.

'I'm not a bad person. Well – maybe I am, but I'm not a very bad person.'

Silence is always best. I just kept my eyes fixed on hers.

'My husband is not evil. All he did was adjust his taxes a bit too much. Everybody here does it. Greeks don't like tax. They want roads and rubbish collected and hospitals, but they think their tax mostly goes into the pockets of politicians and their friends. Maybe they're right. He got a very long sentence. He can come on all macho Greek male, but he's quite a gentle guy, really.'

I resisted my urge to speak. Just.

'He's in the prison in *Ioaninna*. That's on the mainland. Two men came. They had pictures of him in prison. They said if I didn't help them they would kill him. I don't want to be with him any more but I sure as hell don't want him to die.'

I nodded and went through to the sitting room. There was a bottle of seven-star Metaxa amongst the others on the shelf. Back in the kitchen I put some ice into a couple of small tumblers and poured the Metaxa in. She rattled the glass.

I spoke very quietly. 'What did they want?'

She tasted the brandy with the tip of her tongue. 'They said they needed my flying skills to handle a drone in the darkness. Just *ice*, they said. Diamonds. Who cares about diamonds? I may be a rich bitch but I've never seen the point of diamonds. I didn't like these men. They looked like they were violent. They had guns. They weren't Greek – I'd guess they were Russian or Serbian. They give me money I don't need and don't want. I do what they ask.'

I had to get her to go through what was happening so that I could measure it against what I knew. Standard technique. I know most of what you're doing, so if you tell me a lie about it I'll know immediately.

'Okay. How does it work?'

'Listen Johnny. I don't want my husband to die. If I talk they'll kill him.'

'Maybe. Maybe I'll kill them first.'

'For Christ's sake. I don't want anybody to die!'

'I think we can avoid it. But you must tell me.'

She held the brandy and leaned back against the cooker. My scrotum decided it wasn't on team Tina any longer and began to relax.

'A ship sails by out in the bay. It sends a commercial drone with a load. I take over when it's close enough and land it. I get the cargo and then send the drone back. That's it.'

'What do you do with the cargo?'

'I take it to a building in the village and hand it over.'

'Who to?'

'Stop bloody interrogating me, Johnny! Hear me out.'

I made a placatory gesture.

'I give it to some men at the old hotel in *Agios Stefanos*. Then I go home.'

'Good. What's the cargo like?'

'A couple of foam things like bricks.'

'How much do they weigh?'

'Maybe a kilo or two.'

'That's probably several billion dollars' worth of diamonds. You don't smuggle diamonds by the kilo. Had it crossed your mind it could be drugs?'

She cried. 'I don't know. I don't want to know.'

I gave her a few moments and then said 'I want you to write down your husband's name and the name of the prison.'

'Why?'

'Please just do it.'

She took a notepad stuck to the fridge with a

magnet and wrote on it. 'I want to trust you,' she said.

'Tina – there are only two people you can trust in the world tonight, and that's me and Suzi. I need to make a phone call. Please don't go away.'

I grabbed my phone from the living room and went out beside the swimming pool. Halfway through dialling the connection shut down. Then the lights in the house went off. I thumbed the light on my phone on and ran inside. Tina was already lighting candles in the kitchen.

'Have you got a land line?' I asked. She walked over to a phone on the wall and picked it up.

'It's dead. Welcome to Greece.'

CHAPTER TWENTY-TWO

'Walk slowly with your hands visible,' I said as we came closer to Suzi's house. The entire area was in darkness, but I knew the alarms were all battery-powered. 'Suzi can be a bit trigger-happy.'

We stood outside the door for a minute. Suzi didn't come that way – she came from around the back with an H&K gun in her hand. She dropped her arm.

'Sorry guys,' she said. 'A threesome is definitely not on the cards. What gives?'

'All the power and phones are out. I need the satellite phone. Now.'

'Stay there.'

She went in and came out with the chunky phone. 'Tina - come with me.'

Good job I'd memorised the numbers. It took what seemed like eternity to acquire the satellite link and put the codes in. I made the call and went inside. Suzi and Tina were sitting in the kitchen in candlelight. Suzi had the H&K on the table in front of her in easy reach. She poured some Ouzo into glasses and pushed a bottle of water across to us. I took some more glasses from the shelf and handed one to Tina.

'An explosion's taken out the main power grid for the island,' I said. 'Could be a transformer blowing. Could be sabotage. Too early to say.'

'Those things burst into flames all the time,' said Tina.

Suzi turned to me. 'That's true, but maybe not true. Where are you at?'

'Tina's being blackmailed. She thinks she's flying diamonds or maybe drugs in under duress.'

Suzi laughed, but her fingers were always close to the gun. 'Tina,' she said, 'Johnny is hopeless with women.'

Tina leaned forward and said 'I wouldn't say he's hopeless. He's actually pretty good.'

'Oh, I see. Silk knickers and see-through bras and he'll believe any old crap.'

'There's no point wearing a see-through bra if you haven't got anything worth seeing.'

I coughed – politely, I hoped. 'Ladies,' I said, 'This is an emergency. Can we focus, please?'

They settled down. Part of me was disappointed in a childish way. Were they having a cat-fight over *me*?

Suzi went all professional. 'Have you told Tina what she's bringing in?'

'No. I've told you what she believes she's bringing in.'

Suzi went across the room and retrieved a slip of paper. She put it on the table in front of Tina.

'I tested the bag in room twelve at *Artemis*. That, *my dear*, is a life-sentence.'

Tina stared at it. 'What's *Semtex*?' she said. 'It rings a bell.'

Suzi smiled in the way an executioner probably

does as he cleans his teeth before leaving for the gallows. 'It's plastic explosives. You are a terrorist.'

Tina's face seemed to collapse. She turned to me. 'Please Johnny – tell me this is not true.'

'Sorry, Tina. It's true.'

The lights came on. Thirty seconds later my phone rang. I said 'Bandit' and listened for a while. 'Okay.'

They were staring at me. 'Circuit-breaker blew,' I said, 'Cause unknown.' Confronted with two strong women my primal instinct was to back down and hide in a corner. That's just the way I am. I can only overcome it by being arrogant and, on a good day, professional. Oh, the leadership training. I must be decisive but sensitive. I must give praise before pointing out faults. I must never exhibit confusion. Maybe that's all true, but it's not what I am. I gave it a shot.

'Suzi,' I said, 'Back off. Tina – you will fly to *Pre-veza* and land at exactly eleven-thirty. You will taxi to the general aviation area and wait. You will then be given further instructions. I will go with you. Suzi will run the bar in Artemis, so she'll need the keys. Understood?'

'Why?' she asked.

Suzi went to say something, but I put my hand up to stop her. 'You have to make a decision, Tina. You'll see.'

Suzi nodded and brought some cheese and biscuits. She put a bottle of ginger beer from *Arillas* on the table. But she carried the H&K with her.

*

It was grey and overcast at the airport. We went to the Olympic Air desk as before, but this time we were told to take a seat. Almost immediately a tall man with a crew-cut came in and said 'Please come with me.' He led the way to an office and gestured to the chairs opposite his desk.

He introduced himself. 'I'm the head of security at the airport,' he said, adding 'Both civil and military. You have a take-off slot at ten-fifty.'

'I need to file a flight plan,' Tina said.

'No need.' He handed some sheets of paper to her. 'Already filed. You will not deviate from this unless an emergency occurs. Understood?'

Tina scanned the flight plan and nodded.

He went on. 'There are two F-35 fighters at *Preveza*. They have cannons and air-to-air missiles. Bear that in mind if you feel like going off course.' He turned to me and pushed a Glock and some ammunition clips across the table. 'You will load this now, and keep it loaded until you are back in this office. If Mrs Alexaki does not comply you will shoot her. You will hand this gun back immediately you return.'

'If I shoot her I might as well shoot myself,' I said. 'I can't fly the fucking thing.'

'Every job has its bad days, Mr Almond.'

This time we walked to the plane. An armed policeman walked five yards behind us. I knew exactly what was going on. This was pure theatre, designed to scare Tina shitless. It was sure as hell working on me. I had no idea whether there were fighters at *Preveza* or not – I thought they were all busy playing dangerous war-games with the Turks, but what did I know? I tried to focus on the amusing idea of Suzi handing out coffees to sun-burned Brits and discussing mosquito bites, but it didn't work.

The cop and I watched Tina do her walk-around inspection of the Cessna, and then he gestured for me to climb in first. I did up my harness as she pulled herself into the left-hand seat, and we put our headsets on. The engine burst into life at ten forty-five, and we taxied to the halt-point in front of the runway near the terminal, then to the left and did a one-eighty on the round bit at the end.

We took off with plenty of runway to spare and soared over Corfu Town heading northwards. Suzi banked the plane steeply to the right. I tightened my grip on the Glock, but we levelled off when the compass in front of me was pointing more or less to the south. We reached five thousand feet and she put it into autopilot.

'Would you do it, Johnny? Would you really shoot me?'

I didn't say anything. I mean, what the hell could I say? There were mountains on the left and sea to the right as soon as we passed the southern tip of Corfu.

'That region over on the left is *Epirus,*' she said. 'Up in those hills is the oldest theatre in Greece. Past that is the town of *Ioaninna.* It has a beautiful lake and some very interesting caves. Pyrrhus, the king of *Epirus* was one of the greatest military commanders of the ancient world. Although he won a major battle against the Romans, he lost almost all of his army, his generals and his friends. Hence the phrase *a Pyrrhic victory*.'

'I know how he felt,' I said. 'Been there many times.'

'Don't you find it odd,' she said, 'that one day we're making love and the next you're prepared to shoot me?'

'Don't you find it odd that a wealthy woman who went to a posh private school is smuggling Semtex into Greece.'

'How do you know I went to a private school?'

'If you don't want people to know, don't leave glossy alumni magazines on your coffee table.'

'Oh. I'm not very good at it, am I?'

'Tina – They want you to be good at one thing and one thing only. The less you know the better, and when they don't need you they will shoot you without a second thought. As far as they're concerned you're just a clever donkey. The last thing *I* want to do is shoot you. But if you do anything that makes me think for a second that you are not a donkey but a general, I will shoot you. Understood?'

After a pause she said. 'Johnny, I really like you. Suzi is in love with you. But she is tough and selfish. I want to prove to you that maybe – just maybe - I could love you as much or more. Will you let me?'

'How?'

'I want to show you how you could shoot me and not die yourself.'

'Go on.'

'You see this button on the control column? You press that and you can speak to air traffic control. Don't keep the button down or you will jam the frequency. I'm going to turn off the autopilot. Don't worry. Okay?'

She switched the autopilot off.

'Now – I'm going to take my hands off the control column. Feel free to point the gun at my head.'

She put her hands in her lap. The plane bobbed for a moment and settled in a nice even flight.

'You see?' she said. 'The plane is trimmed and it will fly itself. There a bit of side wind from the north east so we will start to drift to the left. Put your feet gently on the pedals and just put a little bit of pressure on the right peddle.'

I did, and the plane started to turn to the right. 'I said gently.'

I eased off on the pedal and the plane resumed its course. 'Good,' she said. 'That's the rudder, like a boat. Now put your hands on the control column and just ease it to the right, only a tiny bit.'

The plane banked a little to the right, and she told me to do it to the left to correct and get back on track.

'Need to go up? More throttle. Here. Need to go down? Less throttle. Got it? You're flying the plane,

Johnny. If you shoot me dead, just keep it level and talk to air traffic control. They will help you land. Now you're going to put the autopilot back on – here.'

'Tina…' I said.

'What?'

'…nothing.'

She followed the instructions on the radio. You can bet that I was listening carefully. We turned to the east over some low hills. 'We're flying down-wind,' she said. 'We want to land into the wind if we possibly can.'

Isn't it strange? Those moments when I'd had the plane under my control were really great. It was like a snort of cocaine.

'Tina – When this is over, will you teach me to fly?'

She turned to me and said, 'Please excuse my language, but if we come out of this alive I will teach you to fly and I will fuck you like you'll never forget.'

She brought the plane in to a perfect landing. There were two fighters on the taxiway as we passed. We turned off the runway and headed for a series of low hangers. The high hazy cloud had vanished and the sun was out. A woman with two table-tennis bats waved them up and down, and when she crossed them over her head Tina turned off the engine and did something to engage the parking break. When the propeller stopped turning another woman walked out of the hanger in front of us. Sophia.

We climbed out of the plane and walked across the tarmac to her. Tina didn't see the police marksman on the hanger roof, but I did.

I walked behind them, as I should, gun in hand, and we went into the shadowy interior of the hanger. There were two police cars side by side. Sophia gestured to me to stop, and Tina to go forward. Sophia and I stood side by side as a tall man with dark hair tinged with grey stepped out of one of the cars. He took Tina in has arms and hugged her for a long time.

'I had to call in a lot of favours to get this,' Sophia said. 'Tina's ex is going to a safe house and his sentence may be re-evaluated, depending on what happens. Her story has some credibility. He was seriously attacked two months ago and nearly lost the sight in one eye. It's not good now.'

'Did he say who did it?'

'No. He refuses. But we have suspicions.'

'How many neo-Nazis are there in that prison?'

'At least five. But full marks.'

'They tell her they'll kill him if she doesn't co-operate. They tell him they'll kill her if he grasses on them. Very neat. He's safe. So how do we protect her?'

'That's your job.'

'We need more troops.'

'I can't spare them – not until we know the target. There are many targets, Johnny.'

'They'll know he's been moved.'

'We move prisoners all the time. We've covered it. Keep everything normal and just observe. I mean it.'

'Normal is not the word I would choose.'

'I'm Greek. My English is limited.'

'Your English is perfect, and you know it.'

'Inspector Almond. Your injury has lowered your self-esteem. You feel less powerful. Now is the time to up your game. Don't let these women run you. Take control of them.'

I laughed. 'Do you know the English expression "herding cats"?'

But I knew she was right. I was reacting and not controlling. It hadn't occurred to me that my self-esteem was as damaged as my hand and I should have paid more attention to the people in the para-Olympics who broke records with half a leg or played Rugby in wheelchairs or ski-jumped when they were blind and said *fuck this, I'm not giving in* and drove themselves through the pain and just did it.

We watched Tina's husband get back into the car and the two cars driving away in convoy. Tina stood watching them go. Then there was an ear-shattering roar and first one then the second of the F-35s screamed away into the sky and vanished.

As the roar faded Sophia said "We only have ten of those. That'll give you an idea how important this is.'

Tina walked towards us and Sophia went to meet her halfway. She put her arm around Tina and they spoke for a while, the sound of their Greek like cracking wood or a hissing kettle. A couple of ground staff were checking the plane. One of them handed a sheaf of paper to me and they left and went towards what must have been their office, their Hi-Viz jackets and white-striped black trousers shining in the hazy sunlight.

Tina's face was stilly shiny with tears as she walked around the plane. She said nothing. When we climbed in she studied the paper-work and clipped it onto the door beside her. She spoke only to the tower on the radio and then started the engine. She moved the control column up and down, right and left, watching the screens in front of her and looking up at the wings above. A red *Jet2* plane came in to land and a couple of minutes later I heard the *Cleared for take-off* message from the tower. The plane bounced about as we lifted off and headed out to sea, levelling off at four thousand feet – I was getting quite good at some of the instruments.

Eventually, she spoke. 'Spiros wants me to say thank you. Actually, so do I.'

'How was he?'

'He can hardly see with his right eye. They sent me a photo back then when they did it. They said it was nothing to what they would do if I didn't co-operate. I don't think they were lying, do you?'

'No. He's safe now.'

'I want to kill them, Johnny. Will you give me a gun?'

I ejected the ammunition clip from the Glock, and the round that was loaded, and held it out to her.

'You don't just need a gun, Tina. You need the ammo and you need the training. But I still don't know if you're going to work with us.'

'Don't be stupid! I'll do whatever it takes.'

'Either you just leave it to Suzi and me – which is fine – or you join the team. Which is dangerous.'

'It has a price. Did you ever read Milton?'

She half-laughed. 'We took a stab at *Samson Agonistes* at school, but it was incredibly tedious and anyway our English teacher preferred drama.'

'The last line is *And calm of mind, all passion spent*. Samson has given up the world and pulled the temple down around him for a higher purpose. That's what we have to do.'

'I didn't know policemen read poetry.'

'Some people find it surprising we can walk and talk. The thing is, Tina, you're angry – very angry…'

'That's an underestimate.'

'…and anger is a weakness. Well – let's say there are two kinds of anger – hot anger and cold anger. Hot anger can make you do stupid and dangerous things. Did you play lacrosse?'

'Yes.'

'Right. You have a weapon. Somebody trips you up. You see red and you hit them hard with your stick. They probably don't shoot you, but you get expelled. That's hot anger.'

'So - what's cold anger, Johnny?'

'You don't react when she trips you. You merely protest to the referee. Then you plan carefully and go to the joke shop after school. You buy lots of itching powder and you wait until the next match. In the changing room you put loads of itching powder in her knickers and after the match you watch her getting more and more twitchy and worried looking until she has to leave the class, red-faced, with her privates on fire. Rumour has it the school has sent her to the STD clinic. She is humiliated. That's cold anger.'

Despite it all, she laughed – properly laughed.

'The thing is,' I said, 'we're trained to use cold anger, Suzi and me. You're not. We're trained to use guns. You're not. Suzi is trained in deep cover – I'm not and you're not. You want to kill now. We want to get them rounded up and locked up and suffer for a long time. Which means, if you are with us you have to do *exactly* what I say even if you disagree. No arguments. Immediately. Can you do that, Tina?'

'I can try.'

'Try is not good enough. Our lives may depend on it. Will you let me *try* to land this plane?'

'No. You don't know how to.'

'Right. So what you do now is fly us back and drive us to *Agios Stefanos*. Those are my instructions. I will give you and Suzi more instructions later.'

We were flying towards the north-east. Ahead,

two islands came into view – a small one and a bigger one, both green. 'What are those islands?' I asked.

'The larger is *Paxos* and the smaller is its little sister *Antipaxos*. Very good for wind-surfing. Talking of which, have you noticed anything about the plane?'

'It's jerking about a bit.'

'Correct. The wind is stiffening down the Adriatic. The *maistro* is coming. We can't go sight-seeing in a gale-force wind.'

Sure enough, the sea below was starting to speckle with white horses of spray. The plane dropped and rose and the engine noise increased and subsided as the autopilot corrected. It was getting bumpy. This wasn't like being in a nice fat jet loaded with duty-free and bacon sandwiches. We were low enough to see a ferry bucking and dipping in the increasing swell with its wake a patch of pearl smeared out across the sea behind it. The skies were darkening and the cloud was getting thicker.

CHAPTER TWENTY-THREE

She was quiet for a while as she drove, probably digesting the latest developments. In the valleys there was a stillness in the trees, but as we crested the mountains the cypresses and olives were lashing in the wind.

'Tell me about Suzi,' she said suddenly.

'Ah,' I said. 'Suzi. She's intelligent bordering genius at some things, particularly computers and technology. She's physically and mentally strong. She can run fast, and she's a good shot. She's competitive. She's reliable. She's professional.'

'Okay – That's not telling me about her. That's reading out her CV. What do you think of her as a person? Does she have any faults or is she just perfect as far as you're concerned? Bearing in mind that you are obsessed with her.'

There is just one traffic light between Corfu Town and the north of Corfu, in a village on a hill. We waited behind a truck loaded with sheets of marble.

'I am not obsessed with her.'

'Piss off, Johnny. You think she's Superwoman and Helen of Troy on gas. You positively quiver when you're near her.'

Considering fifty percent of the human population is women, do we really need psychiatrists? Women seem to come equipped to dissect people without even thinking about it.

'I'll let that go. All right – Suzi is not good with people. She's probably some way up the autistic scale. She can be pretty nasty. I'm not sure she means it, really, but she doesn't suffer fools, and from her viewpoint most people are.'

'Including you?'

'Obviously.'

'I don't think so, Johnny. I think she's very much in love with you. She's just not very good at showing it. But she's also not brilliant at hiding it.'

'Look – She has her weaknesses. I taught her to swim, here.'

Tina laughed. 'I think you'll find that she was a junior swimming champion when she was at school. Oh my God, you two are a perfect match! She wants you to be stronger, you want her to be weaker, and neither of you can be up-front enough to say it or do it. Honestly, it's like watching fourteen-year-olds on a first date.'

The marble truck ground its way up the hill when the lights changed.

'If you see all this, why did you sleep with me?'

'Maybe I had itching powder in my knickers.'

*

When we walked up the path past the pool at *Artemis* Suzi was handing out ice-creams with a fixed smile on her face that reminded me of a corpse in a mortuary with *rigor mortis*. The canvas canopies of the sunshades over the sunbeds were swaying and twisting as the wind picked up and the inflatable animals in the water were rammed together at the shallow end like a protective ring of wagons in a Western. Tina went around the pool and lowered the canopies. I went to the bar.

'Any chance of a coffee?' I asked.

'If you want a fucking coffee you can fucking-well come around here and make the fucking coffee for your fucking self.'

'Oh dear,' I said. 'I'll take that as a No.'

I went through the building and into the bar and started to make coffee with one hand – maybe a bit more incompetently than was strictly necessary.

'Oh, for fuck's sake!' Suzi said, and grabbed the filter-holder and the coffee from me.

'Stop it, Suzi,' I said. 'I can see you've had a bad day, but I've been up in the air at five thousand feet in a little plane with a potential killer and a couple of state-of-the-art fighters just behind us with their missiles armed and ready to shoot us down.'

You know that wasn't strictly true; I know that wasn't strictly true – but it was close enough to make the point.

'And?' she asked.

'Mission accomplished.'

'Great!' she said. 'So how did you two celebrate? Did she give you a blow-job at five thousand feet?'

I was about to say *you've never done it even at ground level* when the sensible part of me kicked in, despite the fact that a tiny bit of me – well, actually, quite a large bit of me - was marvelling at the naked jealousy, the like of which I had never seen before.

One by one the residents were retreating to their rooms. Plastic beer glasses were blowing around the poolside in flurries as Tina went around collecting the rubbish and stuffing it into the bins on little posts which had somehow escaped the notice of the tourists. Let's face it, Suzi was crap at running a pool bar.

'Well, that's running a holiday apartment off your Shirley Valentine bucket-list,' I said. Then I briefed her on developments. Tina finished tidying up the pool and joined us.

I told them what was going to happen next. They didn't like it.

*

I had a shower and a kip. All the tension of the day had somehow migrated down my arm and into my right hand. Suzi went back to her villa to get supplies. Everything had to look normal. Normal is quite hard to achieve when you start thinking about it. I'm sure actors train for years to seem normal. We had to look as though we were relaxed and having a good time when we were as tight and wound-up as a guitar string that's about to break.

We were munching our way through various varieties of *gyros*. I was having grilled pork with *satziki* and chips wrapped in *pitta* bread in a paper cone, at Y*iannis Grill* halfway up the high street, when Tina's phone rang. She looked nervous as she answered it and held a finger over her lips to tell us to keep silent. She left the table and went down on to the road. We could hear her shouting into the phone in Greek and gesticulating. Nobody around seemed bothered – shouting into phones is pretty-much average communication around here.

She was furious when she came half-running back onto the terrace. She tried to keep her voice down as she said 'They want a pick-up at eleven-thirty. I told them they were mad. The wind is far too high for the drone. I might get it in but I'll never get it back.'

Suzi put her hand on Tina's arm. 'What did they say?'

'They said, this is the last one. They said if I don't do it they will shoot me.'

I was about to say *they were almost certainly going to shoot you anyway* and thought better of it. Instead, I said 'We might be able to turn this to our advantage. Do you think you can land the drone on the beach? Really?'

'It's going to be difficult. Almost impossible. You saw how the wind kicked the plane around today. Now imagine something much smaller. It'll blow around like a leaf.'

'Understood. But can you do it?'

'I don't have much choice, do I?'

Suzi said 'There's always a choice. It has to be up to you.'

'We'll be close,' I said. 'And armed. Suzi is a really

good sniper.'

'Suzi doesn't like me! Why should she care?'

'Suzi is a professional,' I said.

Suzi took umbrage at this. 'Am I allowed to speak for myself? Actually, I do like you, Tina. What I don't like is you getting all competitive over Johnny. We'll talk about it when all this is over. But until it is, I will blow the head off anybody who aims anything bigger than a pea-shooter at your unspectacular tits. Okay?'

My turn. 'For fuck's sake you two. Shut up and listen.' They did. 'Suzi, do we have night-vision goggles in the kit-box?'

She nodded.

'Good. Here's what we do.'

*

Suzi drove the jeep down past *San Stefano Travel* and onto the beach. The sea was roaring in with white lines of racing surf foaming up the sand. The wind-blown water was forcing its way into the little lagoon at the end of the stream, where a broken-down wooden bridge rocked in the usually-calm water. She stopped the jeep beside the stream and killed the headlights. The H&K machine pistols were in the seat-well beside my feet, together with a mean-looking sniper rifle with a long telescopic sight. We pulled our night-vision goggles on and the world turned from darkness to an eerie green light.

We crossed the stream at a steady speed and headed along the beach right at the edge of the sea to avoid the sunbeds. Spray blasted across the windscreen. 'Quieter,' I said, and Suzi changed up the gears and slowed down. The lights of a luxury yacht bobbed in and out of visibility out to sea. We passed beside the lights of the hotels and tavernas on our right and at the boat hire station we turned around the fragile structure, its Greek flag lashing about in the wind, and Suzi pulled-up facing back the way we'd come.

The wind was whining through the electricity cables as we got out of the jeep and sand was blowing writhing snakes across the beach. We held the guns at the ready. The lights from Romanza glared in the goggles high above us and fifty yards ahead. Now everything depended on Tina.

At eleven forty-three exactly I pointed a big torch out to sea and before long the drone appeared jumping and swinging from side to side in the wind. It held over the sand for a few seconds then dropped onto the beach and shut down. She'd given us very clear instructions and we knelt beside the drone, unfastened the latches on the cargo bay, and felt inside. It wasn't what we were expecting. But I held the bay door open as Suzi slapped some tiny trackers to the package, and we closed the doors and stood back. After another thirty seconds the drone started up and flew away up the tide-line.

As soon as we'd jumped into the car and shut the doors Suzi said 'She's bloody good. I'll give her that.' The car moved slowly at first and then faster back to the car park, beside the sunbeds with their flapping collapsed brollies. At the stream she turned the headlights on and we took the night-vision gear off.

'Best guess?' I asked.

'Detonators.'

'I agree. It's end-game time.'

We drove up the road from the beach, past *Margarita's* supermarket, up the incline past *Olympia* and down to the carpark opposite *The Little Prince*, where a handful of people were chatting and enjoying their last drinks, sheltering from the wind behind big plastic screens. Suzi parked the Jeep nose towards the road for a quick take-off, and I connected the hardened iPad to the powered whip-antenna in the back of the Jeep and turned on the tracker software.

Tina's car wasn't where we expected it to be, heading down the hill to the abandoned hotel. It was going the other way, up the hill towards *Avliotes*, completely the wrong direction.

'They've changed plans,' I said. 'Let's go!'

The Jeep accelerated round the bend and up the main drag. There weren't many people about, and Suzi wasn't bothered about the speed limit or the tyres. The coloured dots on the iPad screen were appearing and disappearing as we went in and out of signal, but we were catching up fast. At the top of the hill the road shallowed off as it approached the old village, and we could see her tail-lights and indicator as she turned left up a steep hill before the village proper.

'Lights off, goggles on,' I said. Suzi slowed down and I handed her the night-vision equipment. It was dark and windy as she killed the headlamps, and I slid my goggles on. We came to a junction. I just caught sight of Tina's tail-lights up to the left through the side-window.

'What's up there?'

'I don't know. Haven't been up that road.' She drove up the hill. The moon was a ghostly light green with dark green clouds going passed incredibly fast. Tina's tail lights vanished.

'She's parked,' I said. 'We'd better stop here. Suzi pulled in and turned the engine off. I reached into the back and grabbed my rucksack. She did the same. We climbed out and closed the doors as quietly as we could, although the wind was howling like a wounded hyena, downwind to us, and there wasn't much chance of being heard. I passed Suzi a light-weight radio headset and put mine on. Suzi had explained that these used advanced encrypted digital stuff and hopped frequencies a thousand time a second. I didn't really give a shit if we were live on Radio One, but we could whisper and hear each other clearly.

High above us up the hill was a looming building with a cross on the top. Tina's car was parked at the bottom of a long flight of steps leading up to the church. The doors and boot were open.

We moved quietly on the fringes of the road and walked along the edge of the car-park, machine pistols in hand.

'Safeties off,' I whispered.

'Got it.'

'Circle to the right. I'll take the left.'

There probably wasn't much moonlight without night vision but we knew better than to chance it. Suzi vanished into the shadows and I moved left. I used the zoom on my goggles. 'There's nobody in the car. Cover me – I'm going up.'

They'd built this church on the highest point. There were maybe forty steps up to the building. There was no cover. I went up slowly, the H&K tightly gripped in my left hand. The bell-tower reached above me towards the sky and its two bells were swinging in the wind. I moved into the gloom where the church blocked the moonlight.

'Clear. Come up.' I held the gun on my crooked right arm and watched until she came over the top of the stairs in a crouch and reached the wall beside me.

'Let me go first,' she said.

'Okay.'

I followed her around the front of the church and down the side, keeping in the shade. We circled the church but there was nobody there unless they were inside. We checked. The door was locked. We skirted the fringes of the hilltop platform on which the church was built. Then I saw something not too far away. A sudden glare of moonlight lit up a huge dish wgich was angled up a little and northward out to sea.

'What the hell is that?' I whispered.

'Oh shit. That's military radar. Built in the Cold War, probably. It's pointing straight up the Adriatic.'

We didn't need to say any more. We examined the low wall around the church, and there it was – a distinct path leading down into the trees. Suzi was over the wall like a monkey and I followed more slowly.

'Trees,' I said. 'Take the right.'

We flanked the path, one on each side, moving carefully through the undergrowth until we reached the perimeter fence of the radar station. There were two of them, and Tina. She was carrying the hold-all. One of the men – looked like the one from the abandoned hotel – was behind her holding a gun. They stopped. The second man was smaller, but carrying a package of some kind. Tina put the hold-all down and the smaller man reached inside, took something out and began fixing it to the package he was holding.

We got as close as we could. The small man was holding a mobile phone, from the look of it.

'Are you thinking what I'm thinking?' Suzi whispered.

'Suicide bomb. Using Tina.'

'Shall I take them out now?'

'Wait.'

The red mist came down. I wanted them. I wanted to stick some rounds through their heads. I moved forward and fell over a root. My finger hit the trigger and the automatic fired three quick shots. These guys were pros – they hit the ground instantly and wriggled into cover. Then the big man fired, but not at us. Tina fell across the hold-all. I rolled away through the brush. Suzi had vanished, but so had the targets. There was a searing pain in my right hand.

The smaller man made a mistake. He ran. Two sharp cracks sounded from away to my right – double-tap – and he hit the ground.

'Good shot, 'I said. 'We need to take the other one alive if we can.'

He'd vanished. I slid on my stomach as close to the edge of the trees as I could. I desperately wanted to get to Tina, but that was open ground around the perimeter fence. I stood behind a tree, scanning left and right, right and left. That's when he hit me from behind. I heard the crunch of his feet and ducked but a he got a glancing blow across my shoulder with his gun. I dropped to my knees. He laughed quietly and I felt the tip of the barrel against the back of my head.

He grunted, and the gun went off. I was still alive. When I turned he was face-down in the little branches and Suzi was kneeling on his neck. He was strong and fighting. We wrenched one arm up his back and then a second.

'Keep still or I'll fucking shoot you!' Suzi yelled. He didn't. 'Johnny – take my knickers off.'

'What?'

'You never did understand that, did you? Reach

up my dress and pull my knickers off. Now!'

I slid my hands up her legs and pulled the knickers down. She moved one leg and then the other, still trying to hold the big bald struggling man. 'Make a rope and tie his hands.'

I rolled the panties up and twined them around his wrists, my own right hand aflame with agony as he fought me. Never knew knickers were that strong. I pulled the cloth tighter and tighter until his arms were trapped. Suzi reached down and tightened it some more.

'Do you speak English or Greek?' she said.

'Both.'

'I'm going to get off your neck. One move and you're dead.'

She stood up. He made to stand and she shot him through the thigh. He screamed.

'Want another one?'

He shook his head. 'Go, Johnny,' she said, loud in the headphones in my ears. 'I've got this.'

In the green vision of my goggles I could see that Tina was bleeding from her shoulder. I ripped her sleeve off and took a medical patch from the rucksack. 'Hold that tight with your other hand,' I said.

Another shot cracked behind me in the trees and another scream.

'I told you,' I heard Suzi say in my headset. 'The next one's in your balls, big man.'

I helped Tina get up. I didn't want to stay near the hold-all a second longer than necessary.

Twenty yards down the clear area around the fence we went into the trees a little way and I sat her propped up against one. My mobile had no signal, so I took the satellite phone out of my rucksack and made the call. The wind had died down a little and the leaves above us were merely swaying and not lashing. My right hand was alternately very painful and then numb.

'Is Suzi all right?' she asked.

'She's armed and dangerous and has a man lying at her feet,' I said. 'She's probably very happy.'

'Fuck off, Johnny!' a cheerful voice said in my headphones.

It was forty minutes until we heard the sound of the helicopter. It came in black and noisy and settled on the other side of the buildings. Four dark shadows ran along the road out of the installation and up the fence towards us, guns held at the ready. When the soldiers reached us, I pointed in the direction where Suzi was standing guard. Then a wave of pain seared my arm, and I fainted.

It was deafeningly loud in the attack helicopter. The big man was strapped in a seat, his legs covered with blood, and a soldier sitting on the seat facing him with what looked like an AK-47 pointed at his heart.

*

Sophia pushed open the door of the treatment room in Corfu's hospital and came in without asking, followed by Suzi. Tina's shoulder was strapped up and she was a bit pale, but calm. My right arm was in a sling. When my gun went off the bullet had missed my hand, but the blast from the gun had seared its way right across my old wound. It wasn't hurting much because they'd pumped me full of morphine and put local anaesthetic on it. The dawn light was rosy in the window.

Sophia surveyed the wreckage that was us, and turned to Tina. 'That was extremely brave, Katerina Alexaki. Normally you would not hear what I'm about to say and technically I should not tell you. But I will. Please don't repeat it.'

Tina nodded, and Sophia continued. 'There have been seventeen terrorist events in Greece, Albania, Romania, Croatia. A coordinated attack designed to destabilise Greece and the Balkans. Very few succeeded because of good intelligence. You will notice that Serbia is not on the list. The fascist elements responsible have been rounded up and are being interrogated. They were supported by Russia.

'Here in Kerkyra there was a bomb in the telephone transmitters on Mount Pantokrator, but the monk had been replaced in the monastery by Special Forces. The attackers are downstairs in the mortuary. The bomb didn't go off.

'The man with the unusual handcuffs is about to be interrogated. You'll be pleased to hear that I have instructed that they are not to give him any anaesthetics or pain-killers.

'The oligarch's ship you identified was a little damaged when it refused to divert to our harbour.

An F-22 fighter took out its engines with a missile and it is currently having a rather unpleasant experience at the mercy of the storm.

'Thanks to you three, the tracking station between *Avliotes* and *Peroulades* identified a number of unusual ship movements further north in the Adriatic. This is classified. Under *no* circumstances will you repeat this: the Italian navy is surrounding a Russian submarine near *Bari*. We believe it is carrying weapons to support illegal military regimes.

'You deserve praise. You will not get it publicly, I'm afraid. But I have a message from the President of Greece to you: *Greece loves heroes, and you are heroes. On behalf of all freedom-loving peoples we salute you.*'

She smiled – not her characteristic mean smile – a warm smile. 'Tragedy has been averted, for now. Next time, Inspector Almond, try to shoot the bad people and not yourself.'

She walked out and the door clicked behind her. The sun was rising to the east and the wind had slowed to a stiff breeze. Suzi came across to me and kissed me on the forehead. Then, to my amazement, she did the same to Tina, and then sat beside her and put her arm around her.

'Up the Gooners,' she said.

EPILOGUE

The physiotherapist ladies in their oh-so-smart casual wear finished and left me alone. Was that snow on the tips of the Swiss Alps I could see through the clinic window, or just clouds? They brought me lunch – fresh wild salmon pan-fried in butter, salad and sauté potatoes. I flexed the fingers of my right hand around the knife and cut into the fish with something like joy.

The surgeon came in with a clip-board, grinned, and made a flourishing signature. 'That, Monsieur Almond, is your release.'

'I don't know how to thank you.'

'Your hand is better than it ever has been. You have made medical history – surgery plus stem cells. Your case will appear – anonymously, of course – in many major scientific papers.'

I punched the air. With my right hand.

*

At four-o'clock the nurse came in and said 'You have a visitor,' and went out, leaving the door open. My visitor walked in, wearing a soft lemon dress and coloured bangles on her wrists. Her hair was like gold thread in the Alpine light.

'Hi, Johnny,' she said.

'Hi Suzi.'

I was stretched out on the bed, like the lazy slob I was. She came over and stood beside me.

'There's a taxi outside. There's a plane at the airport. Guess who the pilot is?'

'The Red Baron.'

'Near enough. First I have to check out your new hand.'

I held it up and wriggled my fingers.

'Impressive. Do you remember what we did when I needed something to tie the big man up with?'

I nodded.

'Do it!'

'Really?'

'Yes, really Johnny.'

I ran my hand up her leg under her dress until I reached her waist.

'You aren't wearing any knickers,' I said.

'Correct,' she said. 'Now just remember that and we'll have a very nice holiday.'

AFTERWORD

I very much hope you enjoyed reading this novel. I'm nearly eighty years old at the time of writing, and I've had a long career writing screenplays for television. It's while since I wrote a novel, and I simply wanted to get that off the bucket-list before I sink into total senility. I really had fun writing Private Eye episodes for TV. Writing is a lonely job, but on location while shooting goes on it's a pleasure having a drink with the actors and the crew, or sometimes being an Extra. Johnny Almond has elements of Hazell and Boon and Shoestring. Bob Banks-Stewart, who originated Shoestring and Moon and Son, once said to me "Fine - but beef it up a bit!" Almond is certainly that. The village of Agios Stefanos NW is a real place. The only fictional building is Artemis, because I could not have the owners of real places doing what Tina does. The restaurants and the people in them are genuine. You can go there and eat the same lovely food. You can swim in that blue sea and walk along the same sandy beach. That's what Douglas Adams did: he wrote the novel version of A Hitchhiker's Guide to the Galaxy in the village long before it became the place it is today. If you fancy a package holiday, TUI and Jet2 both operate there. TUI call it San Stefanos. Jet2 calls it Aghios Stefanos. If you prefer to do your own thing, check out CorfuSelections.com where you'll find plenty of details of independent apartments, villas and hotels, or contact San Stefano Travel at http://www.sanstefanos.co.uk.

Johnny has his own page on Facebook with pictures of the village and other fun stuff. https://www.facebook.com/Almond-Co-111926344834385

Printed in Great Britain
by Amazon